FROM THE
NANCY DREW FILES

THE CASE: An abducted child, a dead suspect, a desperate race against time.

CONTACT: When Nancy first met Jeremy Wright, he foresaw his own kidnapping.

SUSPECTS: Edwin Wright—A powerful attorney who may have decided to take the law into his own hands to get custody of his grandson.

Kamla Chadi—Jeremy's teacher. Her close friendship with his mother may have turned her into an accomplice.

Arnie Beyers—An ex-con working at Wright's estate, he may have found a profitable new reason to return to his criminal ways.

COMPLICATIONS: A family fighting over the future of a child is more than complicated—it's tragic and it's dangerous!

Books in The Nancy Drew Files™ Series

Available from ARCHWAY Paperbacks

The NANCY DREW Files™
105

STOLEN AFFECTIONS

CAROLYN KEENE

AN ARCHWAY PAPERBACK
Published by POCKET BOOKS
New York   London   Toronto   Sydney   Tokyo   Singapore

This book is a work of fiction. Names, characters, places and
incidents are products of the author's imagination or are used
fictitiously. Any resemblance to actual events or locales or persons,
living or dead, is entirely coincidental.

AN ARCHWAY PAPERBACK *Original*

 An Archway Paperback published by
POCKET BOOKS, a division of Simon & Schuster Inc.
1230 Avenue of the Americas, New York, NY 10020

Copyright © 1995 by Simon & Schuster Inc.
Produced by Mega-Books, Inc.

ISBN: 0-671-88196-5

First Archway Paperback printing March 1995

10 9 8 7 6 5 4 3 2 1

NANCY DREW, AN ARCHWAY PAPERBACK and colophon
are registered trademarks of Simon & Schuster Inc.

THE NANCY DREW FILES is a trademark
of Simon & Schuster Inc.

Cover art by Cliff Miller

Printed in the U.S.A.

IL 6+

STOLEN
AFFECTIONS

Chapter

One

"I CAN'T WAIT to see Kamla again," Nancy Drew said to her father, Carson, as they pulled into the parking lot of the River's Edge Day School. "She really loves her teaching job, and she credits you with getting it for her."

Mr. Drew smiled. "That's complimentary, but not exactly true. All I did was see that her immigration status was in order. It was a nice change from the criminal work I usually do. She got the job on her own merits. She's a smart young woman." He reached over and patted his daughter's hand. "Like somebody else I know!"

Nancy undid her seat belt and flipped her long reddish blond hair over her shoulder. "Does this look careerish enough for Career Day?" she asked her father as she got out of the car. Nancy was wearing a new electric blue linen suit that showed off her slim figure and highlighted her blue eyes. The short skirt and long one-button jacket were complemented with a matching silk blouse.

She and her father had been invited to come to the school that afternoon to talk to the third-grade class. It was Career Day, an annual event in which prominent people from River Heights visited and discussed their occupations with the elementary school children.

"You look perfect," said Carson, beaming at Nancy with pride. "I'm so glad you could come with me. I want the kids to know that teamwork is important. The best lawyer in the world can't win a case without someone like you researching the facts."

They entered through the heavy double doors of the elegant private school, its red brick walls barely showing through the heavy covering of ivy. The school had once been the residence of a wealthy doctor in River Heights. Here, Kamla Chadi, a twenty-three-year-old native of Bombay, India, had obtained her first teaching position after graduating with honors from the University of Michigan with a degree in education.

Nancy had met Kamla through Carson, and had introduced her to her friends Bess Marvin and George Fayne. Through the summer the three young women had included Kamla in some of their activities, taking her to the River Heights Street Fair and the raft races and waterskiing on the river. But when fall came, each had become busy with her own plans.

Kamla met the Drews in the principal's office. She shook hands with Mr. Drew and gave Nancy a hug.

She was dressed in her native sari, a length of cloth in bright reds and oranges that covered one shoulder and set off her dark hair and complexion. Her long hair was drawn back with a red silk scarf, and she wore delicate silver bangles on her wrists.

"Thanks so much for coming," she said. "The children are very excited about meeting you." Kamla grinned and shook her head. "If only I could bottle their enthusiasm." Her dark eyes twinkled mischievously. "They just spent an hour with an accountant." She lowered her voice. "I don't think any of them are ready to choose that career! But they are really looking forward to meeting a criminal attorney and a private investigator." She turned to Nancy as they walked down the long hall to her classroom.

"Are we still on for an early dinner tonight?"

"Yes. George has my car today," Nancy replied. "She'll pick us up here at four."

"Good thing," Kamla replied. "Mine can't be relied on to get us anywhere. I had to hitch a ride this morning. I'm furious at that mechanic at the garage. Three hundred dollars and it still won't run!" She dismissed the topic with a wave of her hand. "What about Bess? Will she join us?"

Nancy shook her head. "No, Bess left for Florida yesterday to visit her aunt. She'll come back with a good tan, and we'll all be shivering."

"And she'll have a new boyfriend to talk about," Kamla added, her eyes twinkling. "Bess falls in love very easily."

"That she does," Nancy answered with a grin.

The children were chattering excitedly when the trio entered Kamla's room. She held up her hand for silence, and immediately the room was quiet. Nancy could tell that the children loved and respected their teacher.

Kamla's third-grade class was small—about fifteen students. Their desks were arranged in a circle, and two extra chairs had been added for Mr. Drew and Nancy. Kamla's desk, at the front of the room, was neatly stacked with papers.

The time went quickly. After Carson and Nancy had explained their work, the children bombarded the father-daughter team with questions. Mr. Drew was asked about one of his more sensational cases—a robbery in which hostages had been taken—a case that had received a lot of publicity nationwide.

One sandy-haired, stocky boy raised his hand. "Is a hostage like being kidnapped?" he asked.

"Yes," Mr. Drew replied.

The boy, freckle-faced and precocious, had

asked several probing questions during the hour and appeared to be extremely bright.

"I know about kidnapping," he volunteered.

Carson smiled. "Good," he replied. "The more you know about it, the better." He looked at the eager faces around him. "How many of you know how to protect yourselves against kidnappers?"

Hands shot up in the circle.

"Don't get into a car with a stranger."

"Don't talk to people you don't know."

"Don't take candy from people."

"Walk home from school with a friend."

"Don't let strangers into your house."

"Yell real loud."

"Very good!" said Carson.

The boy who had started the conversation put his chin in his hands and frowned, as if he was weighing the information.

When the bell rang, signaling the end of the school day, the children called out their thank-yous and filed out.

Mr. Drew consulted his watch. "I think I may have enough time to get to the courthouse before it closes," he said. He looked over at Nancy. "Thanks for your help. I couldn't have held their attention without you. Are you sure George is coming to pick you up?"

Nancy nodded. "Positive."

"Okay," Mr. Drew said. "Then I'm on my way. Have a nice dinner, ladies."

"We will," Kamla said. "Thanks for coming." She turned back to the room with a puzzled look on her face. "Jeremy," she said, "is something wrong?" The boy who had asked about kidnapping was still sitting at his desk.

Jeremy grinned. "Nope. I had some questions for Nancy, but they're sort of private."

"Oh," Kamla said in an understanding tone. "I'm sure Nancy won't mind answering your questions . . . but first, I'd better introduce you." She turned to Nancy. "This is Jeremy Wright. You may know his grandfather Edwin Wright. He's a prominent criminal attorney here in River Heights. Jeremy is living with his grandfather while his dad is on a scientific expedition in the Amazon."

"I've heard my father speak of Edwin Wright," Nancy said. She held out her hand to Jeremy. "I'm pleased to meet you, Jeremy. What questions did you want to ask me?"

"Well, I guess they're not really questions," he said. "But I didn't want to say anything in front of the other kids."

"Say anything about what, Jeremy?" Nancy smiled at him as she sat down at the next desk.

"Well, I mean it's all good stuff about not talking to strangers, and yelling loud, not opening the door, and not taking rides from people, but I'm not going to do any of those things, and I'm still going to be kidnapped. Really soon."

Kamla stopped cleaning off her desk and

walked over to Nancy and Jeremy. "Why do you think that, Jeremy?" she asked with concern.

"Because I just know I am. Because I'm a good private investigator."

"Remember what I said to the class?" Nancy said gently. "Private investigators deal with facts. Do you have any facts to prove that?"

"I really do," Jeremy said. "I heard them planning it. None of the things you talked about is going to happen. No strangers, no candy, no cars. But it's really going to happen!"

"Tell me more about this," Nancy said.

Jeremy held up his hand to signal "stop." "What's the password?" he asked.

"What do you mean?"

Jeremy gave her an I-can't-believe-you're-asking-me look. Patiently, he explained. "For access to the information superhighway, you need to give the password."

"Oh, dear," Nancy said. "The password?"

"That's it!" Jeremy shouted. "Password!" He leaned forward and whispered. "But it won't work the next time. The password keeps changing."

"Okay," Nancy said. "I understand the need for secrecy. But I'm on the highway now, right? So you're going to give me the information."

"Right!"

Nancy heard the door open and glanced over. George had entered the room and was standing quietly by the door, not wanting to interrupt.

But her appearance distracted Jeremy. He peered around Nancy and waved at the newcomer. "Hi," he yelled. "I'm Jeremy Wright."

"Hi!" George replied. "I'm George Fayne."

"But you're a girl," Jeremy said. "Girls aren't named *George.*"

"This one is," George replied, covering a grin with her hand. "Good to see you again," she said to Kamla. She lowered her voice. "Am I interrupting something?"

Kamla shook her head. "No, it's okay," she said softly. "Jeremy had some questions for Nancy. I wouldn't be surprised if he's asked her for a job. He told me this morning he was already at work as a private eye!"

"Sounds like a live wire to me," George said.

Kamla was about to speak when Jeremy stood up and pushed some books into his backpack. "I've got to hurry," he said. "Darcy's waiting and she'll be mad."

Kamla smiled. "See you tomorrow, Jeremy."

"Okay," he replied brightly. "That is, if my grandfather doesn't have me kidnapped during the night!"

Chapter

Two

JEREMY PUSHED open the door with his elbow and dashed down the hall, yelling, "Darcy-Arcy, wait for me!"

"What was that about?" George asked Nancy.

Nancy frowned. "I'm not sure," she replied.

Kamla was standing rock-still, her face drained of color. "What did he tell you?" Kamla asked. "What did he say about his grandfather?"

Nancy shrugged. "Just what you heard."

"Overactive imagination?" George asked.

"He's one of my brightest students," Kamla said. "Very creative." Her deep brown eyes looked worried. "But he usually creates stories in fantasy worlds—about monsters and robots. This is different. This is very real. And I don't think he's making it up."

"Wright . . . Isn't he the kid with the biologist dad and the movie star mom?" George asked. "I read an article about the parents. They're divorced, right?"

Kamla nodded. "Yes, that's the family."

"Let's go," Nancy said. "We can talk about this at dinner. I'm starving!"

At dinner, the girls chattered excitedly about their recent activities. The evening was fun, but Nancy could tell when they dropped Kamla at her apartment that she was still worried about Jeremy Wright.

The next morning Nancy researched some records for her father at the courthouse and then went home for an early lunch. Hannah Gruen, the Drews' housekeeper, had gone shopping, so Nancy kicked off her shoes and sat in the kitchen, reading the paper and eating a sandwich and enjoying the quiet. It was so quiet, in fact, that when the phone rang, she jumped.

"Kamla!" she said, after finding out who was calling. "Aren't you at school? What's wrong? Jeremy's not in class? Well, I'm sure there's a good explanation. Yes, I remember what he said yesterday, but that doesn't mean he's actually been kidnapped. Of course I'll help you check into it. Look, George and I will come by and pick you up after school. Okay, three-thirty in the parking lot."

Nancy hung up the receiver and stared at the

phone. She remembered that when she and her father had been guiding Kamla through the red tape for a work permit, once in a while Kamla would jump to an erroneous conclusion. But Nancy had never heard her friend sound panicky before.

At 3:30 sharp, Nancy wheeled her blue Mustang into the lot at River's Edge Day School. She had picked up George and briefed her about Kamla's call on the way. It was a gorgeous bright and sunny March day, with the hint of a breeze and the promise of spring in the air.

"You said yourself that she jumps to conclusions," George said. "And she seemed to be especially fond of Jeremy." She lifted her sunglasses and looked over at the entrance to the school. "Here she comes. What's she carrying? It looks like a billboard. And she doesn't seem upset—she's got a big smile on her face."

Nancy breathed a sigh of relief. "Hi," she yelled, as Kamla approached the car. She was wearing a different sari under her coat, and Nancy thought of how the native dress made the tiny woman look exotic and just a bit mysterious. "You're feeling better." It was both a statement and a question.

"A little," Kamla said, coming up to the driver's side. "I'm still worried about Jeremy, but look at what his classmates made for him. I said I'd deliver it after school." She held up a huge card made from two sheets of art board hinged together and decorated in vibrant colors, with Get Well, Jeremy!! in big letters on the front.

"And look," she said, opening the card. Inside there were individual messages and pictures drawn by the children in her class.

"Jeremy will love that!" Nancy exclaimed. "But tell me—is he sick?"

"His grandfather called the office and said he had strep throat," Kamla replied. Her tone of voice suggested doubt. "He seemed perfectly well yesterday. Delivering the card will give me a chance to see for myself if he really is sick."

"I'm sure there's nothing to worry about," Nancy said gently, "but that's a good way to ease your mind." She swung open the car door and took the keys from the ignition. "However, Ms. Chadi," she continued, smiling, "your humongous original piece of art will not fit in this car. Let's lay it down flat in the trunk."

Kamla put the card in the trunk and climbed into the backseat. She leaned against the soft upholstery as Nancy expertly steered onto the main road and headed for the exclusive section of River Heights where Edwin Wright lived.

"I'm glad I have you for friends," Kamla said. "Sometimes I get homesick for my family. Not that I don't love it here in the States," she added quickly. "I do. But sometimes I feel overwhelmed."

"In what way?" George asked, turning in the front seat to look at Kamla.

"Oh, just a pileup of various things," said Kamla, rolling her soft brown eyes and giving George a wry look. "My car isn't working, and now they say it will cost *five* hundred to repair. And I got a notice yesterday that my school loan payment was overdue . . . and now Jeremy's disappearance."

"Well, you can't say he's disappeared until you're sure," Nancy chided her. "I know you're thinking about what he told you yesterday, but kids tend to make up stories. And anyway, Jeremy said his grandfather would kidnap him, but Jeremy's already staying with Mr. Wright."

"I just don't think it's a story," Kamla said, with a sigh. "It could be a custody plot on Wright's part. Too often, people tend to discount what children say."

"Not everyone," George protested.

"No, but a lot of them do."

Nancy pulled into the curving driveway in front of the Wright mansion and parked in front of the house. Immaculately groomed foliage surrounded the imposing red brick building. Shady oak trees and tall pines dotted the rolling lawns and neatly clipped hedges, and flower beds bordered the path to the house.

"I think we took a wrong turn," George quipped. "This has got to be a national park."

Nancy smiled. "It sure looks like it," she agreed. "Let's get the card out," she said to Kamla, patting her arm reassuringly.

Kamla returned her smile. "I'll feel better the minute I see Jeremy," she said.

The trio got out of the car, and Nancy opened the trunk so Kamla could retrieve the card.

"Somebody's watching us," George said, frowning. "I saw a shadow at that front window."

"Good," said Nancy. "That means somebody's home."

They walked to the massive front door and rang the bell. The door opened instantly. A heavyset man, about fifty-five, with a ruddy face and gray-streaked sandy hair, stood in front of them.

"What do you want?" the man asked. His tone was abrupt and uncordial. Kamla backed away a step.

Nancy recognized Edwin Wright from seeing him at the courthouse.

"Good afternoon, Mr. Wright," she said, extending her hand. "I'm Nancy Drew. This is my friend George Fayne . . . and I believe you know Jeremy's teacher, Ms. Chadi."

Forced into shaking hands with Nancy, Wright mellowed a little and nodded abruptly at George, but he ignored Kamla completely.

"Ms. Chadi has brought a gift for Jeremy from his classmates. A card that they made," Nancy continued. "May we see him?"

Edwin Wright cleared his throat. "No, I'm afraid that won't be possible."

"We'd just take a few minutes," Nancy persisted.

"No, that's not possible," Edwin Wright repeated. "Jeremy is ill. He's sleeping. He has strep throat and a high fever, and Dr. McColl says he is not to have visitors."

"But the card—" Nancy said.

"I'll see that he gets the card," Wright said, reaching out and taking it from Kamla. "Thank you for your concern, Ms. Drew, Ms. Fayne. Goodbye." He firmly shut the oak door in their faces.

"That man desperately needs to take a class in the social graces," George said, making a face at the closed door. "Talk about getting the bum's rush . . ."

Nancy smiled at George's humor, but Kamla was standing rigid, staring at the door. "He wouldn't even acknowledge me," she said slowly. "I hate to think of Jeremy growing up in his house."

"Well, he certainly wasn't the model of graciousness," George said. "Why was he so rude to you?"

"Because he knows I'm a friend of Jodi—Jeremy's mother."

"Let's go and get something to eat, and we can talk about this," Nancy suggested.

"Great idea," George said. "I do my best talking with food in front of me."

THE NANCY DREW FILES

"You poor, weak thing," Nancy replied, taking her arm. "May I help you to the car?"

"Wait," Kamla said, smiling at their banter. "While we're here I want to check something." She walked around to the side of the mansion and stared up at the second story.

"That's Jeremy's room," she said, pointing to a wide window with a balcony in front. "But the drapes are closed."

"Have you been here before?" George asked.

"No," Kamla said. "But one of my class projects is called My World. I have the children draw their homes and tell what they can see from their rooms. Jeremy said his room had a balcony and that he looked out at a big oak tree with a ladder up the side, leading to a tree house. That's got to be it," she continued, motioning toward an oak with rustic board steps nailed to its side.

"Well, it may be his room, but we're not going to see much through those curtains," Nancy said. "Let's go over to the Village Inn. It's close by and quiet, and it's too early to be crowded. I want to hear more about Jeremy's mother."

Traffic was heavy, and it took twice as long as it usually did to get to the popular restaurant.

When the three had settled in a comfortable back booth at the inn, Nancy turned to Kamla. "Now," she said, "tell us about Jeremy's mother."

"I first met Jodi Fontaine through my father, who's an executive in the motion picture industry in Bombay. The American producer of the film Jodi was starring in was looking for a certain setting in India, and my father helped to find it.

"My father took me to the set to meet Jodi. I spent a lot of time with her while she was in India, and we corresponded when she returned to California. Jodi convinced me to come to the United States for my schooling. She's been like a big sister to me."

"I'm impressed," George said. "I wouldn't mind having Jodi Fontaine for a big sister. What's she really like? She gets good press, but you never know how much is true."

"She's wonderful!" Kamla said. "She's generous and loving and compassionate. Always doing things for people. For all her fame, there's not an arrogant bone in her body."

"What happened to her marriage?" Nancy asked. "Or don't you know?"

Kamla nodded. "Well, the man she married was a scientist. Their worlds were too far apart," she said. "He spent his time in the laboratory; she spent hers on a soundstage. He was always trekking off to do field research; she was always filming on location. It was a sad case of two nice people getting married and finding out that they had little to share with each other."

"And Jeremy?" Nancy asked.

"He seems fairly well adjusted to the split. The parents have both worked hard to help him. They have joint custody, and they both love him a lot.

Jeremy spends the school year here in River Heights with his father, and holidays and vacations with Jodi in California. Only right now his father is doing research in South America, so he's been with his grandfather. Jodi wasn't happy about that."

"Why?" George asked. "Don't she and Edwin Wright get along?"

Kamla shook her head. "Not at all!" she said emphatically. "Mr. Wright was against his son marrying Jodi, but he was headstrong and he went against his father's wishes."

"Is it because of your friendship with Jodi that Mr. Wright doesn't like you?" Nancy asked.

"Mostly," Kamla replied as she picked at her salad plate. "He also looks at me as a—" She paused. "As a foreigner. He's bigoted. As one of the biggest contributors to River's Edge Day School, he tried to talk the board out of hiring me, but the papers had already been signed."

"That rat!" George said.

Kamla nodded. "He doesn't like me, and he likes Jodi even less. He'd do anything to stop her sharing custody of Jeremy. I tell you"—her eyes were sad as she looked at them—"I don't think Jeremy's sick."

"Have you talked to Jodi about Edwin Wright?" Nancy asked.

"Not recently. And I don't want to alarm her unnecessarily about this situation. For all we know, Jeremy could be at home in his bed sound asleep. So far, we have no proof that Wright's broken the law. We can't arrest him for being rude. And if Jeremy's father chooses to leave Jeremy with his grandfather, there's nothing we can do." She shrugged and spread her hands out in a gesture of futility.

"Well, you've got to admit that Edwin Wright takes good care of Jeremy," Nancy said. "I mean, he had apparently taken him to the doctor. Didn't he mention Dr. McColl before he slammed the door?"

Suddenly George sat up straight. "Dr. McColl!" she exclaimed. "I bet that's Steven McColl, the pediatrician. I can find out if Jeremy really has strep throat. I'll call my friend Marlene Otto. She's Dr. McColl's nurse." She looked at her watch. "I may catch her at the office. Sometimes she works late."

George borrowed a quarter from Nancy and left to make the phone call. She was back in a few minutes, and the grim expression on her face told Nancy that the news wasn't good.

"Guess what?" George said, sliding into the booth. "Dr. McColl couldn't have said no visitors for Jeremy. He's been abroad on a medical mission for a month and won't be back till next week!"

Chapter
Three

"SO EDWIN WRIGHT WAS LYING," Nancy said.

"Looks like it," George replied.

"I just know Jeremy's in danger," Kamla whispered.

"We don't know anything for sure, Kamla," Nancy said as she looked over to the hostess station to signal for their check. The restaurant with its charming, rustic country-inn furnishings was beginning to fill up. She looked at her watch. "The dinner crowd is arriving. Let's go and do some checking, okay?"

"How? How can you check when Edwin Wright won't even let us in the front door?" Kamla asked.

"There are ways," Nancy replied confidently. She picked up the check the waitress had brought, then pulled some money from her wallet. The other two did the same. Nancy looked from Kamla to George. "Are you ready to go?"

Walking through the parking lot to the car, Nancy handed George her keys. "George, you drive. Drop me off at the Wright estate and then take Kamla home. I don't want my car to be seen parked outside the place."

"I don't want to go home," Kamla protested. "I'd like to come along and help you with that man. Just because he's got a lot of money and influence in this town, it doesn't mean he can get away with anything!"

Nancy reached over and took her friend's hand. "Kamla, I really do understand your frustration, but this is something I need to handle myself. I promise I'll call and let you know what I find out. But for now let George take you home."

"All right," Kamla said reluctantly. "Sorry I got carried away." An impish grin spread across her face. "What are you planning to do?"

"I'm not sure yet," Nancy replied, grinning back at her. "I'm going to try to get into the place and see if Jeremy is there."

"How are you going to do that? Break in?"

"No, nothing that drastic. But your having pointed out his room was helpful. Maybe there'll be a door open in the back of the house, or maybe Wright will have a change of mind and let me see Jeremy."

"Not a chance," George muttered, and Kamla nodded her agreement.

Nancy didn't think there was much chance of that, either. Edwin Wright didn't look like someone who could be swayed easily once he had made up his mind, and he'd already proved that he was not above being downright rude to stop any visit to Jeremy. Nancy could remember hearing her father say that he was a formidable court attorney when cross-examining witnesses and that he didn't care who was hurt in the process. Edwin Wright's record as an attorney was respected, but Edwin Wright, the man, was not well liked in legal circles.

As they approached the Wright estate, a large dark-colored car pulled out of the driveway, heading in the other direction. George slowed down and pulled over to the edge of the road.

"That's him!" Kamla said as the car disappeared. "That's Edwin Wright's car! I've seen it when he comes to pick up Jeremy at school."

"All the better," Nancy muttered. "One possible complication out of the way. Maybe there'll be somebody at the house who'll let me in." She opened the passenger door and got out. "Give me an hour, and then come back and get me," she said to George.

Nancy stood on the front walk, staring at the rather gloomy mansion. The curtains were open in one of the downstairs rooms, but the rest of the house was dark and heavily draped. Nancy moved cautiously from the front walk to the flower bed and looked through the window.

There was no one in the room, which appeared to be a den or a home office. Bookcases lined the far wall and leather chairs flanked a large desk.

Nancy approached the front door and rang the bell. No one responded. She rang again. If Jeremy was in the house, someone was bound to be there to look after him, she thought. When a third ring brought no answer, she crept from the front of the house to the side. She glanced up at Jeremy's room. The drapes were still closed.

Silently, Nancy moved toward the old oak that housed Jeremy's tree house. She was glad she had changed into jeans and jogging shoes before going to the school to get Kamla.

Dusk was closing in. If she was going to see anything from the tree house, she knew she needed to act quickly. She looked around to see if anyone was watching, and reached for the first rung of the makeshift ladder.

"Nancy Drew!"

Startled, Nancy let go and looked up. The voice was coming from above, but she couldn't see anyone.

"Nancy Drew!"

"Who is that?" she asked.

There was a thump over her head, and a face appeared out of the tree house, at the top of the ladder.

"It's me, Darcy Adams. I saw you yesterday at school."

"I remember you, Darcy," Nancy said, grinning up at her. "You're Jeremy's friend."

"That's right," Darcy said. "His *best* friend. Are you coming up?"

"May I?"

"Yes, you may, but if you're looking for Jeremy, forget it. He's history."

Nancy climbed into the tree house and sat cross-legged on the floor, facing Darcy, who was fiddling with a walkie-talkie. A couple of jigsaw puzzles were stacked on top of some board games in a corner. An unfinished puzzle took up part of the floor space.

"What do you mean, he's history?" Nancy asked.

"I mean he's not here anymore."

"Are you sure?" Nancy asked.

"Positive," Darcy said. "See, we have these walkie-talkies, and when I call Jeremy, I get somebody who doesn't know the password."

"Oh," Nancy said. "What does this somebody say to you?"

"Not much," Darcy replied. "He pretends to be Jeremy with a sore throat, but I know it's his grandfather. He keeps telling me to go home, so I know it's not Jeremy. We're co-owners of this place. He wouldn't tell me to go home."

"Co-owners of the tree house?" Nancy asked.

Darcy nodded. She pushed the antenna in and sighed. "No use even trying now," she said. "Mr. Wright just left. Do you want to help me finish

24

this puzzle? It's hard. It's all sand on one side and ocean on the other, and the colors are all the same. Jeremy's great at puzzles. He started this one yesterday. I wish he was here to help me finish it."

"Darcy," Nancy said, "where do you think Jeremy is?"

"He's probably with Arnie."

"Who's Arnie?"

"Mr. Wright's friend. He's a crook. He fixes TVs. He fixed Jeremy's TV last week."

"What makes you say he's a crook?"

"I don't know," Darcy said with a shrug. "He just looks like a crook to me. And besides, we were up here the other day when—"

"Who's *we?*" Nancy asked. "You and Jeremy?"

Darcy nodded. "Of course! He's the only other person who's ever come up here—except you."

Darcy picked up a pair of binoculars from the floor and trained them on the window of Jeremy's room. "So we were up here the other day when Arnie came to fix the TV, and he and Mr. Wright were standing down by his truck. It's green and yellow."

She put down the binoculars, stretched out on her stomach on the floor, and pointed to the driveway below. "He was parked right down there, and we could hear everything they were saying."

"What were they saying?" Nancy asked.

"Oh, they were talking about Arnie picking up

25

Jeremy and taking him off to a motel for a few days. Jeremy would have a ton of games and puzzles to play with, no schoolwork, and then after a while he'd come home. Jeremy kind of liked the idea." She turned and looked at Nancy. "But I thought it sounded strange—too much like a kidnapping. Like what your father was talking about yesterday at school."

"And you think that Jeremy has been taken away by this Arnie?"

Darcy nodded. "Yeah."

"Well, why didn't you tell somebody?"

Darcy gave her a puzzled look. "Jeremy said yesterday he told you."

Nancy swallowed. "Well, that's true. He did say something about a kidnapping." She paused as she replayed Jeremy's conversation through her mind. He had said that no strangers would be involved. And no bribes. And no strange vehicles. Drew, she said to herself, you blew it.

"What else did Mr. Wright say to Arnie?" Nancy asked Darcy.

"That he'd get the rest of his money when the job was done, and that he should pick up some games and books and puzzles to keep Jeremy amused."

"Wasn't Jeremy scared when he heard that?"

Darcy gave her a look that suggested Nancy had taken leave of her senses. "Why would he be scared?" she asked. "It's an adventure! His grandfather planned it. Jeremy doesn't have to go to school. He doesn't have to clean up his room. He probably doesn't have to take a shower every night. I wish I could have gone, too."

"Oh," Nancy said, smiling as she followed the eight-year-old's logic. She looked beyond Darcy to a thick rope hanging from a branch just above the girl's head. "What's that rope for?" she asked.

"That's our newest home improvement," Darcy said proudly. "Just watch!" She grabbed the sturdy rope with both hands and before Nancy could stop her, pushed off and sailed out of the tree house and over the balcony railing that skirted Jeremy's room. "Cool, huh?" she said, clutching the rope for the trip back.

"Really cool," Nancy said as Darcy swung back to the tree house.

A beeper signal sounded, and Darcy looked at her watch. "Rats. Time to go home. But you can stay as long as you want."

"Thanks," Nancy said. "I may just sit up here and think for a few minutes."

"Fine with me!" Darcy yelled, skittering down the ladder. "See you around!"

Nancy grinned as the small figure ran across the rolling lawn to the large house next door, but she didn't sit long. When Darcy was out of sight, Nancy grabbed the rope close to where it was knotted on the branch and tested it. Satisfied that it would hold her weight, she wrapped her legs around it and swung out over the lawn, skirting the railing, and landed with a thump on the balcony outside Jeremy's bedroom window.

Her feet had barely touched the balcony when a floodlight below flashed on and the angry barking of dogs shattered the evening's stillness. Startled at the vicious clamor, Nancy let go and watched in horror as the rope swung back to the tree, far out of reach.

She was stranded on a second-story balcony of Edwin Wright's mansion!

Chapter

Four

S TAY RIGHT THERE, LADY!" a man shouted.
"This is one break-in you're not going to finish!"

A short, squat man wearing a tan windbreaker
and shorts and a plaid tam was standing beneath
the balcony, looking up at her. He was holding
the leashes of two fierce-looking Dobermans,
who were straining at their leashes, growling and
snarling.

"I'm not trying to break in!" Nancy yelled
down at him. "I can explain!"

The sound of her voice only agitated the dogs
more, and they tugged at their leashes.

"That's what they all say," the man called up
at her. "I can't imagine any good explanation for
you being on my neighbor's second-floor balcony. You just stay put while I go and call the
police."

"No, wait!" Nancy called out.

"Seems like you're the one in a position to wait," the man said. "Let me warn you—these are trained attack dogs. They've got funny names —my wife named them—but in this case names don't mean a thing."

He stared up at her, looking ridiculous with his jaunty plaid hat with its pompom on top and his knobby knees sticking out under his shorts, and Nancy struggled with a powerful urge to laugh.

"Minnie and Mickey here, they mean business. They'll see that you don't go anywhere! They're as military as I am. I'm Colonel Albert Fingal, U.S. Army, retired." He gave a sharp command to the dogs, and their response was impressive. They calmed down instantly, stretching out full-length on the ground below, quiet but alert to Nancy's every move. She decided to take this man seriously.

"No! Colonel Fingal!" Nancy called out as he walked away. "Don't call the police! Please, wait. You don't understand! I know Mr. Wright!"

The man below looked up at her and shook his head. "Sure you do," he said sarcastically. "You just swung in for a cup of tea, right? Funny way to come visiting. I'm going to call the police."

As he spoke, the headlights of a car turned into the curving driveway.

"Here's Edwin now!" the colonel said. "Guess I'll let him handle this." He turned his back to her and waved at the car, which was pulling up to the house. "Edwin! Edwin! M and M treed a lady burglar for you! She swung from the kid's tree house right over to the balcony. Says she knows you."

Edwin Wright shut off the powerful engine and got out of the car. He hurried over to his neighbor and peered up at Nancy, who was standing on the balcony, looking very embarrassed. "It's Ms. Drew, isn't it?" he said in a tone that suggested he knew perfectly well who it was. "I didn't expect you'd be paying a return visit tonight. Is there something I can do for you?"

Nancy glared down at him angrily. "Yes," she snapped. "You can get a ladder and get me down from here." Her angry tone agitated the dogs, who stood up and snarled.

"In due time," Edwin Wright said. "And I'll thank you not to yell. I have a sick child in the house." He turned to his neighbor, who was wrapping the dogs' leashes around his hand. "Thank you, Colonel. It was a stroke of luck that you and the dogs should have been out at just the right time to intercept Ms. Drew." He leaned over and stroked the head of one of the Dobermans, who licked his hand in response. "Sort of like our own neighborhood watch," he said, laughing.

"Glad to be of help," Colonel Fingal replied. "Come on Minnie, Mickey. We'll be moving on now, that is, unless you need me, Edwin."

"No, I can handle this," Wright said. "I'll get a ladder from the garage."

A breeze had come up, and Nancy stood on the balcony shivering, trying to think of how she was going to explain her presence on Wright's property. Keeping one eye on the men as they walked toward the garage, she searched for an opening in the drapery that hung on the other side of the sliding glass door leading to the balcony, hoping for a glimpse into Jeremy's room.

Suddenly, Nancy heard the dogs start to bark again. Nancy jumped back from the window and peered into the night to see what was happening.

"There's another one!" she heard Colonel Fingal yell. "It's your night for visitors, Edwin!"

Nancy watched as the two men and the dogs took off after a figure racing from the back of the house, down the driveway, and toward the road. The figure looked strangely familiar. Nancy leaned against the balcony and smiled ruefully, shaking her head. At least she wouldn't be making up her excuses alone. George would be right there with her.

"Stop where you are or I'll unleash the dogs!" the colonel yelled, the ferocious barking backing him up.

George stopped running and turned to face the men. There was some conversation that Nancy couldn't hear, and then Wright turned around and headed for the garage. He came out carrying a ladder. Within minutes, Nancy was standing on the ground, facing Wright, Fingal, and George.

"May I ask what this is all about?" Wright demanded of the two girls.

"May we go inside and talk?" Nancy asked.

"No, we may not!" he snapped. "We'll talk right out here." He looked over at the colonel, who was hovering nearby, obviously interested in what was coming next.

Wright cleared his throat. "Thanks for your help, Colonel," he said. "I'll take it from here."

"I don't mind staying if you need me, Edwin. Or if you want me to call the authorities," the other man said.

"Thank you," Wright said, "but I'm fine. I know this pair."

Wright waited until his neighbor and the dogs were out of earshot and then turned to Nancy and George. "I am outraged that you would violate my privacy like this!" he said to Nancy. "How dare you come on my property! I want an explanation."

Nancy looked down at the ground before she started to speak, refusing to be intimidated by his courtroom theatrics. Stay cool, Drew, she said to herself, or you won't find out anything. "You're right," she said, looking up. "I apologize. I—we had no right to come here without your permission, but we had a good reason."

"And what might that be?" Wright asked, folding his arms across his chest.

"We were worried about Jeremy," Nancy replied. "Kamla—Ms. Chadi, his teacher—was worried, too."

"Ms. Chadi is a meddlesome busybody who is filling my grandson's head with lies about me. If I had my way, she'd be sent back to Pakistan or Burma or wherever it is she came from!"

Nancy's eyes flashed. "It's India," she snapped. "Kamla Chadi is my friend, and she would never try to influence Jeremy's relationship with you. She has too much integrity. She is very professional!"

"She's not too professional to cozy up to that ex-daughter-in-law of mine!"

"They were friends before Kamla ever came to River Heights," Nancy said. She could feel her temper surging, and she fought for control. "We're not here to discuss Jeremy's teacher and mother," Nancy continued in a calmer tone. "We're here because of Jeremy. We're worried about him. Doubly so, in fact, because you won't let us see him."

"I told you, Jeremy has strep throat. He has a high fever and he's in bed."

"His friend Darcy Adams thinks he's not even in the house."

"How would an eight-year-old know about that?" Edwin Wright asked.

"Well, they apparently communicate from the tree house by walkie-talkie."

Edwin Wright clenched his fists in exasperation and glared at her. "Ms. Drew," he said. "You are going to tell me that the person who talked to Darcy this afternoon didn't know the password. Right?"

"Well, yes . . ."

Edwin Wright spoke very deliberately, very softly, and accented each word.

"That's because I was the person who talked to her, and I don't know the password. I don't care to know the password. I was trying, in a nice way, to get her to stop calling on that noisy contraption. Jeremy was sleeping. I finally took his set and locked it in my study."

"But, Mr. Wright," Nancy said firmly, "there are other reasons we are concerned about Jeremy," she continued. "Yesterday at school, he talked about being kidnapped, and . . ."

Edwin Wright looked furious. "And the day before that he told the gardener that he and Darcy were captured by aliens and taken off to some other galaxy," he said, his voice rising. "And last week he was in a time tunnel going back to the Civil War and he was fighting at Shiloh." His voice dropped to a normal level. "Ms. Drew, you are trying my patience. If I did not have a professional tie with your father, I would call the police immediately and press charges against you and your friend." He looked disapprovingly at George, who stared back at him.

"There's something else," George said. "You

said that Dr. McColl had said Jeremy could have no visitors."

"That's correct," Wright replied.

"But Dr. McColl has been abroad on a medical mission for the past four weeks. And he won't be back to his practice till next week."

Edwin Wright took this information in stride. Nancy could understand why he was known as an unflappable defense attorney.

"Ms. Frame—"

"Fayne," George corrected him.

"Ms. Fayne, I personally did not take Jeremy to the pediatrician today. I was in court all day. My housekeeper, Mrs. Henry, took my grandson to the doctor. My grandson's doctor is Dr. McColl. If Dr. McColl is not in his office, he makes arrangements to have another pediatrician see his patients. If, as you say, Dr. McColl is abroad, I am sure that Jeremy was seen by another doctor." Edwin Wright was speaking slowly and carefully, as if to a not-too-bright child. "He was diagnosed as having strep throat, which is contagious. And he was told *no* visitors. Those are the instructions my housekeeper relayed to me when I got home. I have no reason to doubt her. Now, if you ladies don't mind, I will escort you to your car and see you off my property. And I would ask that you not return."

George had parked Nancy's Mustang at the

side of the road in front of the house, and the girls drove off quickly.

"What an insufferable sleaze," Nancy sputtered. "Imagine him talking about Kamla that way. No wonder she doesn't like him!"

"He's a real prize," George said, raking her fingers through her short-cropped hair in exasperation. "And he's good on the comeback. He had an answer for everything you brought up. That stuff about the doctor and all. Do you believe him?"

"Not for a minute! His answers were all very plausible," Nancy replied, "but the man's whole career has been centered around verbally defending other people, so I'm not surprised that he could make a good case for himself. He's very clever." She looked at George and grinned. "What were you doing at the back of the house?"

"Well, I started out looking for you, not expecting to find you on an upstairs balcony," George said dryly. "Then I decided I'd look around for an unshuttered window to see if I could get a glimpse of Jeremy—which also didn't work. And then I was going to see if a back door or a basement door was open so I could get inside the house, but when those ferocious beasts showed up, I sort of changed my plan."

Nancy laughed at the understatement.

"There is one thing I did notice," George said. "There's a trash can out behind the house. Normally, I don't investigate other people's garbage. But sticking out of the top of the can was that huge card from Jeremy's classmates—the one we delivered this afternoon." She paused, then looked hard at Nancy. "Nan, I agree with Kamla," she said anxiously. "I don't think Jeremy's in that house!"

Chapter

Five

THAT MAKES TWO OF US," Nancy replied slowly. "You see, while Colonel Fingal was reporting my attempted break-in to Edwin Wright, I noticed that the drape on the sliding glass door leading to the balcony was caught on a chair or something in the room. I only had a second, but I managed to see the bed. It was empty and looked as if it hadn't even been slept in."

"So we were right!" George said.

Nancy nodded. "I'd stake my life on it."

"You sound as sure as Kamla," George said. "She hadn't cooled down when I dropped her off. In fact, she was debating whether to call Wright and accuse him of kidnapping or call the police with the same message. Maybe both."

Nancy sighed. "I hope she didn't call Wright,"

she said. "He'd slap a suit against her so fast that she wouldn't know what hit her."

"That's what I told her," George said, "but she wasn't paying much attention. I suggested she take a hot bath and relax, and I promised her we'd call her with an update."

Nancy nodded. "We'll do that," she agreed, "but not until we've talked to the police."

"Is Sam working tonight?" George asked.

"I don't know his schedule. I haven't seen him since we worked on that last case together."

"That was a month ago," George said.

"I know, but Sam is really attractive—maybe too attractive. And I can't just forget about Ned." Ned Nickerson was Nancy's longtime boyfriend, who was away at college.

"Still, it's fun to work on a case with a cute young cop," George said, looking over at her.

Nancy laughed. "You are so right."

Sam Fanelli had been on the River Heights force only a few months, and he and Nancy had worked closely together to solve a case of harassment and attempted murder. A smile flickered at the corners of Nancy's mouth as she thought about Sam's shy grin, his deep bass voice, and his wonderful sense of humor. She felt herself blush, remembering one special afternoon when Sam had wrapped his strong arms around her, holding her tight as he gently kissed her.

Nancy wheeled into the parking lot beside the police station. Her heart beat a little faster when she noticed Sam's familiar beat-up compact car parked in one of the slots. He was working that night. You're here on business, Drew, she told herself. You're acting like some lovesick seventh grader. Besides, she thought as guilt washed over her, you have a perfectly wonderful steady, loyal, loving boyfriend in Ned. But then Nancy's mind drifted to the pretty blond Ned had introduced to her after his chemistry class one day when she was visiting the Emerson College campus. His lab partner. Erika something-or-other. And it occurred to Nancy that she hadn't heard from Ned in over two weeks.

"Are we waiting for sunrise?" George asked.

Nancy rolled her eyes. "Just thinking," she said, swinging the car door open. "Let's go in."

When Nancy and George entered the building, they saw a woman officer on duty at the front desk and approached her.

"My name's Nancy Drew. I'd like to talk with Detective Fanelli, if he's available."

"I'll buzz him," the officer said. She picked up the phone and punched in a number, then spoke quietly into the receiver. When she hung up, she turned to Nancy. "You can go on back. It's the third door on the left."

Nancy and George hurried down the hall. But before they reached his office, Sam came into the hallway to greet them.

"Nancy Drew! Best partner I ever had!" he quipped, giving her a bear hug.

Nancy blushed. "Well," she said, "you haven't had that many partners!"

"Sure. Not many, but not one of them as talented or as pretty as you."

George cleared her throat loudly, and Nancy wriggled free.

"Sam," she said, "I want you to meet my good friend George Fayne."

"It's my pleasure," Sam said, extending his hand. "What brings you two down here tonight?"

"Can we talk privately?" Nancy asked.

Sam's eyes twinkled. "How privately?" he asked. Before she could answer, he motioned them through a doorway. "My office is a tight fit. We'll be more comfortable in the conference room." The small room had a rectangular table and six chairs, and Nancy and George seated themselves side by side, across from Sam.

"What's up?" he asked. "You look serious."

"I am serious," Nancy said. "I want to report a missing child. His name is Jeremy Wright."

Quickly, Nancy recapped the events of the last two days, starting with Jeremy's announcement in the classroom that he was going to be kidnapped, and ending with her unauthorized visit to Edwin Wright's estate and getting trapped on the balcony.

"Sam," she said, looking into his sympathetic brown eyes, "I just know that Jeremy Wright is missing. And I think his grandfather is responsible. He's a rude, despicable man, and he seems to hate anybody who gets at all close to Jeremy." As she spoke, Nancy's voice trembled with emotion.

Sam stared at her for a long minute, then he spoke.

"What's your involvement with this, Nan?" he asked bluntly. He shoved his chair back and stood up. His forehead furrowed, and he pushed his hair back from his face.

Nancy looked down at the table, realizing that she had sounded extreme in her condemnation of Edwin Wright.

"Well, Jeremy's teacher is a friend of mine," she said. "That's how I happened to be at the school the day he talked about being kidnapped."

Sam grunted. "Stay here," he said. "I'll be back in a few minutes." He left the room and closed the door firmly behind him.

"That was a quick switch," George commented. "He can look downright mean when he puts on his police officer's face. From moonlight and roses to professional cop without skipping a beat."

Nancy nodded. "I guess I got a little wound up about Edwin Wright. But I don't like that man, and I do think he has something to do with Jeremy's disappearance."

"I'm not sure Sam agrees with you," George said. "He didn't look too thrilled with your monologue." An impish grin crossed her face.

"He's cute though, even when he's grumpy! You have good taste in the looks department. However, my decision on his disposition is still under consideration."

"Oh, George," Nancy said, "I've told you that we're just friends. We only went out a couple of times, and we were working on that case."

"All in the line of duty, right? That greeting he gave you in the hall was a couple of notches up from friendly." George shrugged. "Or maybe that's his version of friendly. How would I know?"

"George, stop it!" Nancy said emphatically. "There's nothing like that between us. We're friends, that's all. Or we were. I'm not sure we still are, from the reaction I got when I started talking about Edwin Wright."

"That did seem to push a button or two. He—" George's comment was interrupted by the door opening.

Sam entered the room and stood at the end of the table. He had a manila file in his hand and a stern look on his face. "I've just talked to the captain," he said. "I wouldn't be able to give you this information without his approval, but because you've worked with the department in the past, Nancy, I have permission to tell you a little bit of what we know on this case."

"Case?" Nancy said, looking wide-eyed at George.

Sam nodded. "You're right about the boy being missing," he said. "However, in my opinion, you're wrong about his grandfather."

George arched an eyebrow, and Nancy could tell she was resisting the urge to comment.

Sam continued. "What I'm going to tell you is to be kept in strictest confidence. The life of Jeremy Wright could be endangered if this information is leaked."

"You know I wouldn't say anything," Nancy said, "and neither would George. Of course we'll keep it confidential. But what is it?"

"In a nutshell," Sam said, "Edwin Wright came to the station this afternoon and reported that his grandson, Jeremy, was missing."

George and Nancy exchanged surprised looks.

"Wright had been warned not to contact the police and not to talk to anyone about Jeremy, or the boy would be killed. So I don't think Edwin Wright is the hateful grandfather you are making him out to be. He seemed to be a very concerned man. Do you realize how much courage it took to come here and tell us? When people try to handle kidnap cases on their own—and without police help—the case almost always ends tragically."

Nancy stared up at Sam, surprised. "It's hard to believe—" she said, but Sam cut her off.

"So now you know why Edwin Wright was so discourteous to you two and your teacher friend when you took the card over, and you know why he was so upset when you ended up on his balcony. He was afraid that you would go off looking for Jeremy, and the kidnappers would get wind of it.

"Another call came in just a little while ago," Sam continued. "It may or may not have been related. The caller threatened to get even with Wright if he persisted in bad-mouthing his former daughter-in-law. As I see it, the family dynamics are not good. In fact, this whole mess may hinge on who has custody of the boy. Particularly with his mother's high profile and financial position, we can't let this get to the press, or we'll have half a dozen copycat callers, all wanting ransom money." Sam hesitated, and then his voice dropped. "I just hope we can get the boy back alive," he said huskily.

Nancy felt a sudden ache in her stomach as his tone changed, and she raised her eyes to meet Sam's. He's doing his job like a good cop, she thought, but with so much compassion, too. Sam's soft brown eyes stared back at Nancy, unblinking, and she resisted a powerful urge to reach out to him.

"Any suspects?" George asked, breaking the spell.

"Yes," Sam replied briskly. "We have two men out right now talking to a possible suspect—a friend of the mother, actually. It is possible that the mother is involved, you know. Custody wars can be messy."

"Have you notified the parents that Jeremy is missing?" asked Nancy.

"We're trying, Nancy," Sam answered. "We haven't had any luck reaching either one yet. They're in faraway places with no phones nearby."

Nancy's mind raced back to her conversation with Darcy about the TV repairman named Arnie. Should she tell Sam about it? No, not yet, she decided. She didn't even know the man's last name.

Sam closed the file folder and opened the door to usher them out.

"Just a minute," Nancy said. "Can you tell us the name of the suspect?"

Sam shook his head. "Nancy," he said, "you know I can't do that. No names until charges have been filed. Right now we're just investigating."

"Thanks, Sam," Nancy said. "We won't say anything."

Sam put his arm around her shoulder and gave her a quick hug as he walked them toward the door. "I trust you," he said. "See you around!"

Nancy and George walked to the car without talking, each thinking over the information they'd just been given.

George slammed the door and fastened her

seat belt. "Are you convinced that Edwin Wright isn't involved?" she asked Nancy as they drove away.

Nancy shook her head. "No," she said. "I think he's smart enough to create a perfect cover. He kidnaps his own grandson and then reports it, so he appears innocent. But at this point the police aren't willing to consider him a suspect."

George sighed. "Right, but they're hot on the tail of a friend of the mother, someone who may or may not have made that call to Edwin Wright. And I'm afraid we both know who that prime suspect is. Are we headed for Kamla's now?"

Chapter

Six

NANCY AND GEORGE DROVE along in silence until Nancy turned the corner of the street where Kamla lived and eased into a parking space across from her apartment building. As she did, a police car pulled away from the curb and drove off.

"If she was upset earlier, imagine how she'll be after being questioned," George said.

Quickly, she and Nancy climbed the stairs to Kamla's second-floor apartment. The drapes were drawn, but the glow from a lamp in the living room showed through. Nancy knocked on the front door. There was no answer. She knocked louder and put her ear to the door.

"She's in there," Nancy said to George. "I can hear her talking."

"Talking?" George repeated. "Who's in there with her?"

"Kamla!" Nancy called out. She rapped again. "It's Nancy and George."

After what seemed like hours, the door opened a crack. "Nancy?" Kamla said. Her voice was hoarse, and Nancy could tell she'd been crying.

"Yes. Let us in, Kamla."

Kamla slipped the security chain off and opened the door. Inside, the small apartment was alive with bright colors. Large tasseled floor pillows in gold and orange silk were heaped in one corner, and a red-and-black tapestry was thrown over the back of the couch. The walls were decorated with ornately carved brass plates, and brass bowls and pitchers graced the coffee and end tables. A set of three thin silver knives with carved handles were mounted over a teak desk in the corner. It was a cozy room, reflecting Kamla's Indian heritage.

"Nice place," George said, looking around.

Kamla sniffed. "Thanks," she said in a whisper. Her eyes were red and puffy, and she blew her nose as she motioned for them to sit.

Nancy looked through the open door to the kitchen. "Is someone here?" she asked. "I thought I heard you talking."

"I was on the phone," Kamla replied. "I was calling Jodi." The words caught in her throat, and she started to sob. "I wanted to tell her about Jeremy . . . and about the police being here." She wiped her eyes and took a deep breath. "But I couldn't reach her. I have her private number, but her answering service picked it up. She's off on location in Mexico. Oh, Nancy, I'm so frightened! What's going to happen to Jeremy? What's going to happen to me?" The tears started again. Nancy moved to her side and put her arm around the diminutive woman.

"Come and sit down," Nancy said, "and tell us what the police said to you."

Kamla sat opposite them on one of the floor pillows and toyed nervously with a silver bangle around her wrist.

"Well, they said they just wanted to ask me a few questions."

"About Jeremy?" George asked.

Kamla shook her head. "No, about Jodi."

"Did they say anything about Jeremy? I mean, did they say he was missing or anything?"

"No, not even when I asked them if he was."

George and Nancy glanced at each other. In her innocent fervor to protect Jeremy from his grandfather, Kamla may have brought suspicion on herself.

"What else did the police ask you?"

"Silly things!" Kamla threw up her hands in exasperation, and the bangle rolled across the floor. George stopped it with her foot and handed it to Nancy to pass to Kamla.

"Nice bracelet," George said, admiring the braided silver.

51

Kamla nodded. "It was my grandmother's."

"What did they ask you?" Nancy prompted.

"Oh, things like, was I in this country legally? Was I able to support myself? And then, before they left, they said they might want to talk to me again, and not to leave River Heights. I feel like a criminal! What's going to happen to my job? Are the police going to talk to the principal about me?"

"They'll check the school for information about Jeremy," Nancy told her. "That's part of their job."

"So he is missing," Kamla said.

"Yes," George replied. "And his disappearance was reported to the police—by Edwin Wright."

Kamla gave her a shocked look. "No," she said slowly. "That man is extremely crafty."

"Yes," Nancy agreed. "Look, we have to go now. We're going to do some checking on our own, and we'll be in touch tomorrow. Get some rest, because worrying isn't going to solve anything."

"I know," Kamla said, standing up and straightening her shoulders in an effort to compose herself. "I've got a big day tomorrow, too. Tomorrow evening is the spring Open House program for parents. Well, let's hope that by then this charade has ended and Jeremy is found safe and sound." She managed a weak smile. "Thanks for coming." She stood at the door and watched as they went down the stairs and across the street to the car.

"She didn't help her case, did she?" George said as they drove off. "She probably shouldn't have let on that she thought Jeremy might be gone."

"I'm afraid not," Nancy replied. "I think our first step tomorrow is to find Arnie, the TV repairman who drives a green-and-yellow repair truck."

"I think you should sign Darcy up as a cub investigator," George said with a laugh. "So far, she's given us our only good leads."

"Right! I'll pick you up at nine."

In the morning, Nancy and George set off with a list of TV repair shops they had copied from the telephone book. At the fourth one they visited, they got lucky.

"Bingo!" George said excitedly as they pulled up in front of the shop. Parked out in front was a green-and-yellow van with the words Uncle Joe's TV Repair Shop printed in black on the side.

"Stay in the car," Nancy said. "I'll go in and see if they have a repairman named Arnie."

As she was entering the shop, one of the servicepeople was leaving. He held the door for her and tipped his green-and-yellow hat. "Morning, ma'am," he said.

"Good morning," Nancy said, smiling at him. The friendly greeting made her feel more comfortable about asking questions.

Once inside the poorly lighted shop, Nancy saw dozens of TVs and VCRs sitting on the floor, helter-skelter, some tagged and ready for delivery back to their owners. Others were covered with dust and had orange For Sale tags on them. Nancy wove her way through to the service window at the back, where a harsh white fluorescent light shone like a beacon over the counter.

"Can I help you, miss?" the man at the window asked. He was wearing the same kind of green uniform with yellow trim that the man she had met at the door had been wearing. The shop's name was embroidered on the pocket.

"I hope so," Nancy said. "I have a friend who brought her set to you for repair."

"Did she have a complaint?" the man asked. "We guarantee our work, you know."

"No, no," Nancy said. "Just the opposite. You see, I have a set that needs repair, and she was so pleased with your work that she recommended your shop and that repairman to me."

"What was his name?"

"Well"—Nancy laughed apologetically—"that's part of the problem. She could only remember his first name. It was Arnie."

"Oh, that would be Arnie Beyers," the man said, grinning at her. "Hasn't been with us too long, but he's good at his job. Of course, all of our

repairpeople are good. But you just missed Arnie
—he was walking out as you were coming in."

"Oh, too bad," Nancy said. "Arnie . . .
Beyers?"

The man nodded. "Right. He spells it B-E-Y-
E-R-S. But you say it like *buyers.* You, know, like
shoppers." He chuckled at his joke. "Do you have
your set in the car? I'll come out and unload it for
you."

"Well, no, I don't, but I'll bring it in one day
soon."

"We send our people out in the field, too," the
man said. "I could have Arnie come by and check
your set right in your home."

"Thanks," Nancy said, dodging around TV
sets as she headed toward the door. "I'll give you
a call and set up an appointment."

She practically ran to the car.

"Found him! Beyers! Arnie Beyers!"

"I could tell by the look on your face," George
said as they sped off. "You looked like the cat that
swallowed the canary."

"He was the man who was leaving as I went
in," she said. "Did you get a good look at him?"

"Sort of," George said. "About five feet ten,
one hundred eighty pounds, big nose . . ."

"Thinning dark hair," Nancy said. "He tipped
his hat when I went through. Did he get into the
repair truck?"

"Sure did," George said. "Where are we going
now?"

Nancy looked at her watch. "Either to the police station or to lunch." She wheeled into a shopping mall and pulled up beside a bank of pay phones. "Have to make a call first."

She jumped out of the car and walked to one of the phones. Her conversation was brief. When she got back into the car, she was smiling.

"I take it we're going to the police station," George said, with an exaggerated sigh, "where we are going to talk with one Officer Fanelli. Am I correct?"

Nancy gave her a sidelong glance. "You are correct," she said. "How did you know?"

"I've never seen you positively glow about going to lunch," George said, then paused. "I hope he's not as grouchy as he was last night."

"He was just doing his job," Nancy replied. "I called because I didn't know what time Sam would come in today, since he worked last night. He's on from eleven to seven."

When she pulled into the parking lot by the station, Nancy took a minute to apply some lip gloss and check her hair.

"Is this a business or a social call?" George teased.

"Both, maybe," Nancy replied. "Do I look all right?"

"You look terrific," George said. "You always look terrific. If you weren't my best friend, I'd probably hate you!"

Nancy laughed. "Come on," she said, getting

out of the car. "Let's see what else we can find out about Mr. Arnie Beyers."

Nancy and George entered the police station and found Sam in his office. He greeted them warmly, with none of the edginess he had exhibited the night before. Nancy quickly explained that Jeremy's friend Darcy had told them about a suspicious TV repairman named Arnie, who had been talking to Edwin Wright just a few days earlier.

"Would you run a check on him, Sam?" Nancy asked. "His last name is Beyers—B-E-Y-E-R-S. I'd really like to know if he has a record."

Sam gave her an I-don't-believe-this look. "Nan, are you going to check out leads from an eight-year-old kid in a tree house? I tell you . . ." He dropped his voice. "I don't think Edwin Wright is involved in Jeremy's disappearance."

"Please, Sam, just as a favor. Ultimately, it may help your case, too."

Sam smiled at Nancy and winked at George. "Pretty persuasive, isn't she?"

George rolled her eyes. "A killer," she said.

Sam laughed. "Okay," he agreed. "I'll run the check for you. But the computer is down right now, so I'll have to call you with the information. Will you be home this afternoon? Say, around four?"

Nancy gave him a big smile. "I will," she said. "Thanks, Sam. This means a lot!"

* * *

At four o'clock George was curled up on the couch in the Drew family room when Sam called. She watched the expression on Nancy's face change from interest to surprise as she hastily made notes during the conversation.

"Well?" George asked when Nancy hit the disconnect button on the portable phone.

"Well," Nancy said. "Arnie Beyers has a long list of aliases. His real name is Jack Farmer—and get this! He was released a year ago from state prison, after serving a three-year sentence for extortion. George, get your jacket. Wright has entrusted his grandson to a crook!"

Chapter
Seven

"W HERE ARE WE GOING, NAN?" George asked.

"To visit Edwin Wright," Nancy said, already at the door. "His office is right by the courthouse."

Edwin Wright's suite was in an imposing new building of law offices that took up almost a city block. Nancy took a ticket from the attendant as she drove into the underground parking lot, and searched on several levels before she found a space.

"This place is worse than the mall," George complained as they were walking to the elevators. "I didn't know there were this many lawyers—or people with legal problems in River Heights!"

"There are a lot," Nancy agreed, pointing to the directory. She ran her finger down the alphabetical list of names. "Here he is! Edwin Wright, Suite 522."

"Do you think he'll talk to us?" George asked as they rode up to the fifth floor.

"I honestly don't know," Nancy replied. "If he really is innocent of any involvement, and if he really is concerned about Jeremy, I think he will. If not, we'll get the runaround."

The two friends walked down the corridor until they came to Edwin Wright's corner suite. It was elegant, with thick blue carpeting on the floors and a sweeping view of the city from the large reception area, which was framed on two sides with plate glass windows. Large, bold abstract paintings in shades of blues and greens adorned the walls, and there were fresh flowers on the reception desk and the coffee table in the waiting area.

"Wow," George whispered to Nancy, as she smoothed her cotton T-shirt over her jeans. "I forgot to wear my formal."

Nancy grinned at the comment and approached the receptionist. "I'm Nancy Drew," she said, "and this is George Fayne. Would it be possible to see Edwin Wright for a few minutes?"

The receptionist looked down at the appointment book on her desk. "I'm sorry," she said. "Mr. Wright's in court today." She hesitated. "I don't see anything in the book. Did you have an appointment?"

"No," Nancy assured her. "We just wanted to talk with him briefly."

"His law clerk is here, though," the woman said. "Perhaps she can help you."

Before Nancy could say anything, the receptionist got up and went into an inner office. She returned almost immediately with a statuesque, striking blond woman fashionably dressed in a leather miniskirt and matching vest, with a soft blue jersey top and chunky gold jewelry.

Nancy thought of George's comment about being underdressed, and shot an impish look at her friend. Neither of them was appropriately dressed for the surroundings.

"I'm Shelley Lawson," the blond woman said, reaching out to shake first Nancy's hand, then George's. "I'm sorry Mr. Wright isn't available, Ms. Drew. Is there something that I could help with?" She looked from Nancy to George with a puzzled expression. "Is it legal advice you need?"

Nancy shook her head.

"Frankly, I wondered," Shelley Lawson said, smiling. "Your reputation as an investigator is well known in River Heights, and of course we have great respect for your father and his fine work as a criminal defense attorney."

"We just wanted to talk briefly with Mr. Wright," Nancy said. "It's a personal matter. I was hoping to catch him before he went home for the day."

"He's been in court all day," Shelley said, looking at her watch. "He may check in before he goes home. Would you like to wait?"

"No, thanks," Nancy replied. "It's not urgent. I'll catch him another time."

"Edwin Wright's no dummy," George said as they walked back down the hall to the elevator. "I always had the idea that law clerks were underpaid. That outfit had to be worth hundreds of dollars."

"She was sharp, too," Nancy said. "Picked right up on my name and knew that Dad was practicing criminal law."

Nancy and George entered the elevator, and Nancy pushed the button for the main floor. "Since we struck out there, let's walk over to the courthouse."

"To find Wright?" George asked, surprised.

"No, I want to check in the Records Section and see if I can find anything on Jack Farmer, alias Arnie Beyers."

"Won't that take forever without a case number?" George asked.

"Sally Moffatt might be able to help. She works in Records, and she's helped me find impossible things before. But we have to hurry. It's almost five, and they'll be closing up."

George and Nancy waited for the light to change and then dashed across the street and into the courthouse.

"Almost closing time, girls," chided the guard at the security desk. "Put your purses on the belt, please. And when you hear the announcement for closing, you'll leave by that other door." He pointed at a door behind him.

"Yes, sir," George called back over her shoulder as she hurried after Nancy.

The Records Section, usually crowded with people needing copies of court orders and litigation proceedings, was empty. A long counter separated the public area from the staff, and on the other side were eight desks and what appeared to be a library-like row of shelves, containing records.

"There have to be thousands of records in here," George said, staring at the files that stretched down to the end of the long room.

"This is just part of them," Nancy said. "The fairly recent ones. The older records are on microfiche stored down in the basement. I can't believe our luck," she continued. "There's Sally!"

One of several women working at computer terminals looked up when she heard her name and hurried over to greet Nancy.

"How can I help you, Nan?" she asked. "You always send me on the most interesting searches."

Nancy introduced George, and then apologized to Sally. "I don't have much to go on this time. I have a couple of names—Arnie Beyers and Jack Farmer." She spelled *Beyers*. Sally scribbled notes while Nancy talked.

"And the approximate date of sentencing would have been about three years ago. The charge was extortion."

"Hmm . . ." said Sally, grinning at her. "You've outdone yourself for lack of information. I don't have much time before we close. I'll skip the stacks and see if I can pull something up on the computer."

She returned to her desk while George and Nancy waited. Static rumbled on a speaker overhead, and a woman's voice announced that the courthouse was closing. All visitors were to leave immediately by the west door. The woman went on to say that the courthouse would be open the next morning at eight o'clock and wished everyone a pleasant evening.

Nancy looked anxiously over at Sally, who was staring at her computer screen. She shook her head a couple of times and then got up and came to the counter.

"Nothing?" Nancy asked. The disappointment in her voice was obvious.

"Not much," Sally said. "We lost some records in a computer shutdown a few months ago—not permanently, but we just haven't had enough support staff to do all the inputting again. So it's getting done in dribs and drabs. The only thing I can pull up on Jack Farmer's case is the attorney of record."

"Who is it?" Nancy asked.

"Edwin Wright," Sally replied. "Sorry I couldn't get more for you."

Nancy grinned at her. "Don't apologize, Sally," she said. "That's a huge help. Bigger than you'll ever know." She turned to George. "Come on, let's go and see if Wright went back to his office."

Sidewalk traffic was heavy when they got back outside, with workers leaving their offices for the day. They hurried across the street and into the spacious foyer of the law building. But before they even reached the elevators, Nancy spotted Shelley Lawson coming out of a court reporting firm's office.

"Ms. Lawson!" she called, maneuvering around a man with a briefcase. "Ms. Lawson!"

The woman stopped, turned around, and smiled when she recognized that it was Nancy calling to her. "Ms. Drew," she said.

"Did Mr. Wright come back to the office?"

"No, he hasn't even called in," she said. "He must have gone straight home. He said this morning that his grandson was sick. I'll be in the office for a while, but I don't expect to hear from him now. I'll leave a message for him."

"Thanks," Nancy said.

Shelley Lawson hurried toward the elevators,

and Nancy walked back to where George was waiting.

"Let's get the car," she said. "He didn't come back."

Traffic was even worse in the underground garage where they had parked than it was on the street. Vehicles were lined up bumper to bumper, feeding slowly out of the structure.

"It's really dumb," George said, "that anybody would build this kind of a complex and not make more vehicle exits. You could get asphyxiated down here at five o'clock from exhaust fumes!"

"You're right," Nancy said. "There's a coffee shop on the main level. Let's go up and have a soda until this traffic jam eases up."

"I guess Darcy is a pretty reliable informant," George said when they were seated. "She's a sharp little girl. She knew the colors of the truck, she knew the repairman's name, and she knew they were talking about kidnapping."

"Which sort of proves Kamla's belief that adults should take seriously the things that kids tell them."

George nodded. "Yeah. Do you wonder if Kamla looks at kids in her class, like Jeremy, for instance, as surrogate family?"

"Probably," Nancy agreed. "I need to call her tonight and see how she's doing."

George rattled the ice in her glass. "Well, I'm done. Shall we go and see if auto heaven has cleared out?"

"Yes, let's. And if you have time, I want to swing by Edwin Wright's place."

"My time is your time," George said as they rode the elevator down to the garage. "But don't expect the welcome mat to be out."

Nancy smiled. "I don't."

The underground garage was clearing, but there was still a line of cars waiting to exit and feed into the street traffic.

"We might as well get in line," Nancy said. She waved her thanks at a motorist who allowed her to back out and queue up ahead of him. Cars inched their way toward the street exit, curving around as they followed the yellow arrows.

"Now I see what the problem is," George said, looking behind them. "There are two other exits to this place, but because of street construction they're both closed."

They were about ten cars away from the opening to the street when Nancy yelled.

"George! Look up there!"

A green-and-yellow van, with Uncle Joe's TV Repair Shop painted on the side, was inching toward the exit. Driving the van was the man who had held the shop door for Nancy earlier.

"It's him all right," George said. "Jack Farmer, alias Arnie Beyers. And there's somebody with him!"

Chapter

Eight

GEORGE JUMPED OUT of the car and zigzagged between the slow-moving vehicles heading for the exit. Nancy watched as George collected a few horn blasts from impatient motorists in her dash to get to the green-and-yellow van. She almost made it, but by the time she got to the ticket booth, the van was pulling out into the flow of traffic on the street. George stared after it for a few moments before wending her way back, a defeated look on her face. The Mustang had moved only about five car lengths.

"I wanted to see who was on the passenger side," George explained to Nancy as she buckled herself in. There was disappointment in her voice. "For a crazy minute, I thought it might be Edwin Wright, but it was some man I'd never seen before."

"It's not a crazy thought," said Nancy. "Was it another repairman?"

"No uniform," George replied. "A suit." She sat silently for a moment. "Why do you suppose Arnie Beyers was here at this building full of law offices?"

"Could be a coincidence. Maybe a lawyer had a broken TV. Or maybe he was just giving the other fellow a ride. Or maybe he had an appointment to meet his parole officer or another attorney here."

George gave Nancy an incredulous look. "Do you really think that?" she asked.

Nancy smiled. "No, I don't. I have a hunch he came to see Edwin Wright and found out—the same as we did—that Wright wasn't in his office."

George leaned back against the seat. "My thoughts exactly. Are you going to tell Sam that Wright was Arnie's attorney?"

Nancy nodded. They were out of the garage now, and she was making her way across three lanes of traffic so she could merge into the main artery that would take them to Edwin Wright's estate. "Of course," she said, "but I want to talk to Wright first." Nancy aimed for an off-ramp, and the rush of freeway traffic gave way to quiet residential streets with expansive lawns and expensive houses. "Who knows? Maybe he'll be more honest about Jeremy today. I'm worried about Jeremy's safety, and he should be, too, entrusting him to a known criminal. But—"

"But?"

"But he may not be any more cordial than yesterday. We'll soon know," she said as she turned onto the road that led to the mansion.

"Speaking of Wright, look!" George was leaning forward, staring at a long dark car that was pulling out of Edwin Wright's driveway. "Missed him again! And he's in a hurry!"

"Hold on!" said Nancy. "We're going to tail him." Instead of turning into the Wright estate, Nancy pressed her foot down on the accelerator, and the little car sprinted straight down the road after its prey. When they came to the crest of a hill, Nancy slowed down. "I want to be close enough to see him, but I don't want him to see me," she explained.

They followed Edwin Wright for about twelve miles on back roads of the county and ended up in the parking lot of a small motel located on a little-used highway that had been pretty much replaced by the interstate.

"Keep an eye on him," Nancy told George. She had slipped her car into a parking space between a pickup truck and a minivan, where it wouldn't be easily seen. "I'm going to the office."

The woman behind the desk was scrawny, with poorly dyed red hair that was, Nancy presumed, supposed to make her look younger than her years. The effect was exactly the opposite, as the flaming shoulder-length hair framed the sagging skin on her thin neck and accented the lines around her eyes and above her lips. She wore a flowered muumuu, and the heavy musky smell of her perfume hung in the air. When Nancy came in, the woman put down the paperback novel she was reading and took off her glasses, letting them dangle from a gold chain around her neck.

"You need a room, miss?" she asked.

"No," Nancy replied, smiling at her. She hoped her hunch was right. "I just need to know which room Mr. Beyers is in."

The woman put on her glasses and thumbed down the names in the register. "Ain't got nobody by that name. Must be staying somewhere else."

Nancy feigned concern. "Gosh," she said sweetly. "I was sure this was where he told me to come." She quickly looked around the small office for an identifying name. A large glass snifter of imprinted matchbooks was sitting on the counter. "This is the Sleepytime Motel, isn't it?"

"This is it," said the woman, "but we ain't got no Mr. Beyers."

"Hmm. Well, maybe the room is registered under his friend's name. Mr. Farmer. Jack Farmer." She looked up expectantly.

"Not is . . . was," the woman said. "Mr. Farmer checked out of unit twelve earlier this afternoon."

71

"Oh, drat," Nancy said. "Well, thanks for your help."

"Don't mention it," the woman said.

Back at the car, Nancy and George compared notes.

"Wright let himself into room twelve with a key," George announced. "He's still in there."

"I'm not surprised. That's the room Arnie checked out of this afternoon. He must have given Wright a key earlier. I don't get it. If they planned to meet here, why did Arnie check out?"

"Maybe we need to ask Mr. Wright," George said, getting out of the car.

"Exactly what I was thinking."

Nancy rapped on the door of room 12, and it was opened immediately. Edwin Wright stared at them in surprise, but said nothing. He stood in the doorway, gripping the doorknob with one hand and the door frame in the other.

"May we come in?" Nancy asked.

He moved aside and motioned them past him.

Room 12 was a typical inexpensive motel room, with a beige carpet, spotted and worn in the traffic areas, a bolted-down TV set on the laminated three-drawer dresser, two lamps, a bedside table, and a small round table with two chairs, above which hung a globe light.

On the round table there was an unfinished jigsaw puzzle, as though someone had left in a hurry, and on the floor, a stack of games. A small basketball hoop and net had been temporarily hung over the closet door, and, lying on the floor, half under the dresser, was a small blue foam basketball. Two empty soda cans were on the windowsill.

No one spoke as Nancy and George stood just inside the door and surveyed the room. Finally, Nancy turned to face Edwin Wright.

"Jeremy was kept here, wasn't he?" she said.

Wright avoided eye contact with her. "That's ridiculous," he said, but his voice wavered. "Why would you think that?" His tough criminal-attorney front was finally cracking.

"Because this room was rented to Jack Farmer, alias Arnie Beyers, a former client of yours, a convicted felon, a man you arranged to have kidnap Jeremy."

"What are you talking about?" Wright blustered. "Where do you get your information?"

"From an eyewitness," Nancy retorted. "A child who—in addition to Jeremy—heard you plotting the whole escapade."

"Who'd believe a child?"

"I would," Nancy said crisply. She walked over and looked at the unfinished puzzle. "You'd better tell me the whole story, Mr. Wright. Where is Jeremy?"

Wright's face turned chalk white, and he sank down on the side of the bed and put his face in his hands. "I don't know," he said. His voice was muffled, and Nancy and George could tell he was barely holding back his tears. "It wasn't supposed to happen like this. Farmer was to bring Jeremy here and keep him amused for a few days. I would go to the police and report him missing, but ask them to keep it quiet." He looked up at them. "Because of my position and because his mother"—hatred oozed from his voice—"his mother is a public figure, a star, who embraces every liberal cause that comes along and picks foreign immigrants for best friends!"

"I don't get it," George said to him, purposely ignoring the crack at Kamla. "What's the point? Why would you arrange to have your own grandson kidnapped?"

Wright lifted his head and stared at her. "Because I want to discredit that woman."

"You were going to frame Jodi Fontaine?" George asked, stunned.

"Yes, and that way my son would get full custody of Jeremy. You see, Farmer was going to tell Jeremy that he was one of Jodi's friends and that his mother wanted him to stay at the motel a few days, and then they'd go to California. Then when I 'rescued' him, Jeremy would innocently tell the police that his mother planned the whole thing."

"I don't believe it," said Nancy angrily. "You would endanger your own grandson to smear his mother. Does his father know about this?"

"No, no! My son had nothing to do with this!"

"If Farmer was supposed to keep Jeremy for a

few days, then why are you here?" Nancy continued.

"Because I called to talk to Farmer, and they told me he had checked out. I got scared. He hadn't even sent me the ransom note yet."

"A fake ransom note that you would blame on Jodi Fontaine and friends, right?" George said furiously.

Wright hung his head and nodded. "I was going to notify the press that I'd paid the ransom and received a motel key, left anonymously at my home. Then I was going to come out here and pick up Jeremy. Farmer would be long gone, of course. He was well paid. And then I was going to file suit against . . . that woman . . . for attempted kidnapping and child endangerment."

"Child endangerment!" Nancy exclaimed. "Where is Jeremy now? Out there somewhere with a convicted felon! Do you understand, Mr. Wright, that your grandson really has been kidnapped? And you're responsible! You need to talk to the police. Again. And this time, you will tell them the truth!"

"I'm sorry, I'm sorry," Wright muttered.

"Sorry doesn't cut it," Nancy told him, barely keeping the disgust out of her voice.

She picked up the phone and punched in a number. "Detective Fanelli, please." She waited impatiently, tapping her foot, until Sam came on the line. "Sam," she said. "I can't explain right now, but put out an APB for Jack Farmer, alias Arnie Beyers. He may be driving a green-and-yellow truck with Uncle Joe's TV Repair on the side." Her voice broke. "Sam, I think he's got Jeremy Wright with him. I'll be in soon."

She hung up quickly and stomped over to the table, sweeping the unfinished puzzle into its box. Then she stacked the rest of the games on top of it and handed the armload to Edwin Wright. "If we ever find Jeremy, he may want to play with these again."

George unhooked the basketball hoop from the door while Nancy bent down to get the ball from under the dresser. She reached in and froze, all her anger dissipating in a rush of fear. Slowly, she reached beyond the ball for a shiny object and pulled out a silver bracelet, the metal intricately woven into a braid. There was no doubt in her mind: The bracelet belonged to Kamla Chadi.

Chapter

Nine

EDWIN WRIGHT STARED at the object in Nancy's hand and then looked up. Their eyes met.

"I knew it," he said huskily. "I knew that foreigner was mixed up in this. She's as bad as the boy's mother. They're in this together. They've been thick as thieves ever since Jodi Fontaine went to India to make that film."

"We don't know that Kamla's mixed up in this," Nancy said. "It's more likely that someone is trying to implicate her. Maybe you and your friends were trying to frame her along with Jeremy's mother."

"Ridiculous!" Wright sputtered. "She even called me last night and threatened me!"

George glanced over at Nancy, remembering

the threats Kamla had made when she took her home and Sam's mention of a second phone call.

"How did she threaten you, Mr. Wright?" Nancy asked.

"Told me I was a poor grandparent and that she knew a way to get even! I taped the calls, if you don't believe me." He reached for the bangle, but Nancy slipped it into her pocket. "You'd better give that to the police, Ms. Drew," he warned, "or you could be charged with withholding evidence."

"I plan to give it to the police," Nancy said, "at the same time that you explain to them your little scheme to blackmail Jodi. We have two stops to make. The first is at your office. I want to see the file on Arnie—that is, Jack Farmer. The second stop will be the police station."

"What makes you think I'd give you the file on Farmer?" Wright demanded.

"Because I think you're concerned about Jeremy, and you need a private investigator on the case, along with the police."

"I know half a dozen investigators," Wright declared. "All top notch."

"I'm sure you do, but it's going to be embarrassing for you to explain to any of them what your role is in Jeremy's disappearance."

Wright hung his head and kept silent.

"Let's go," Nancy said. She handed George the keys to the Mustang. "I'm going to ride with Mr. Wright. Will you follow in my car? We'll make a quick stop downtown and then meet you at the police station."

The underground garage at the law office building was vastly different from how it had been a few hours earlier. Only four or five cars were parked in the slots, their owners upstairs working overtime, Nancy assumed.

They rode up to the fifth floor in silence. A custodian was vacuuming the thick carpeting in Wright's suite when they arrived. Wright motioned Nancy to have a seat and went into an inner office. From her vantage point on the couch, she could see him unlock and open a vertical file. He thumbed through the contents once, and then went through them again. He came back to the waiting area, a puzzled look on his face.

"I don't understand it," he said, over the roar of the vacuum cleaner. "Farmer's file is missing!" He turned to the custodian. "Hey! Hey, you!" The man turned off the machine.

"Yes?"

"Has anybody been in here tonight?"

"No, sir. Just me."

Wright dismissed him with a curt nod and turned to Nancy. "Maybe it's been misfiled," he said. "I'll have my clerk look in the morning."

But Nancy could tell by the way he spoke that he did not think it had been misfiled, any more than she did. Edwin Wright, for all his caginess, had been upstaged—double-crossed by someone smarter than he was.

When they got to the police station, George was in the parking lot, waiting. It was after seven, but Nancy noticed, with some relief, that Sam's car was still in the lot. The case was getting so convoluted that she didn't want to explain it from the beginning to someone new. And she had to hurry. Wright needed to be at his estate when the call for ransom came.

Once inside the station house, Wright insisted on seeing Sam first—and alone. When Wright came out of the office, his expression was somber.

"One of our people will be at your place within the hour to set up monitoring equipment on your phone line," Sam said, shaking hands with Wright as he was leaving the building.

When the door closed, Nancy looked at Sam, exasperated. "How can you be so polite to him?" she said. "Don't you realize that he started this whole mess?"

"He's told me the whole story, Nan," Sam assured her. "He, of all people—with his knowledge of the law—knows he's in hot water. The D.A. may press charges, but right now we need Edwin Wright at home by his phone. Our prime concern is getting Jeremy back safe. And Wright is not a security risk. He's not going anywhere. Now, is there anything else you want to discuss?"

"Yes." Nancy reached into her pocket and pulled out the bangle. "I found this in the motel room, under the dresser."

Sam took it from her and gave her a long look. "Wright told me about this," he said in his low, slightly husky voice. "Nan, I know this is hard for you. I know this might implicate your friend, and I'm sorry. We have a team on the way to the motel now, to dust the room for fingerprints."

Nancy met his gaze. "And a team at Kamla's?" she asked.

"We will have," Sam replied. "I've got a call in now for two extra people. What you've done today has been a big help. Why don't you and George go and get something to eat, and I'll give you a call later tonight and let you know if there are any new developments."

"Okay," Nancy said, a little less defensive.

"Food sounds good," George commented when they got to the car.

"It does, but not yet." Nancy pulled out of the parking lot and headed toward the river road.

"Where are we going?"

"To River's Edge Day School. I want to ask Kamla about the bracelet. Maybe it was stolen. I know she won't be home. Tonight's the spring Open House program for parents."

When they arrived at the school, Nancy and George were stopped in the hall by one of the secretaries, who recognized Nancy from Career Day.

81

THE NANCY DREW FILES

"Ms. Drew! How nice of you to come!"

"I'm sorry I can't stay," Nancy explained, "but I need to talk with Kamla Chadi. It's urgent. Is she in her classroom?"

"No, one of our teaching assistants has taken over her classroom tonight. Kamla called in this morning. She has the flu. I didn't talk with her myself, but I know she must have been terribly disappointed. Her class had worked on a special program for Open House."

"That's a shame," Nancy murmured as she moved toward the door. "Thanks."

Outside, the girls hurried to the car. "What do you make of that?" George asked.

"I'm not sure. But I'm worried about her. Let's get over to her apartment."

"The investigators that Sam called in may be there by now."

Nancy nodded. "But if Kamla reported in sick this morning, they'll be twelve hours too late. And she'd have to be awfully sick to miss that Open House voluntarily."

"What do you mean, *voluntarily?*"

"I don't know. I just have a funny feeling about all this."

"You don't think she's sick."

"No."

"Nan," George said slowly, "do you think that Kamla would kidnap Jeremy to get him away from his grandfather. Maybe take him to Jodi?"

"I honestly don't know. She knows the police suspect her. If she has him, she may be afraid to go to them. But I thought she'd call me." Nancy sighed. "There's also another possibility."

"What's that?"

"We may have two kidnappings on our hands."

"Kamla? But what makes you think that?"

Nancy shrugged. "I don't know. It's just speculation. Part of the plan to frame Kamla as the kidnapper."

"So she could be a victim or a criminal."

"Yes." Nancy pulled the car up to the curb in front of Kamla's apartment building. There were several other vehicles parked along the street, but no patrol cars.

"The police may be in an unmarked car," George said, reading her thoughts.

"Possible."

Kamla's car was not in her assigned parking space, and when they climbed the stairs to her apartment, there were no lights showing through the drawn drapes.

"Nobody home," Nancy said, with concern in her voice. She knocked, but there was no answer. She tried the door, but it was locked. Then she looked around to see if anyone was nearby and fished in her purse for a credit card.

"Keep an eye open," she said to George.

Minutes later the two friends were inside Kamla's apartment. Nancy reached over and turned on a lamp on an end table. The colorful room was neat. She walked through to the bedroom while George checked the kitchen.

"Nothing unusual in here," George said.

"Nor here," Nancy agreed, coming out of the bedroom. "The bed is made, her suitcases are in the closet. It doesn't look as if she left in a hurry. I wonder where she could have gone."

"She's had some phone calls," George said, pointing to the red light flashing on Kamla's answering machine. "The counter says four."

"Let's see if one of them said what time they called. It might give us a time frame on when she left the apartment."

Nancy touched the Rewind button and replayed the last message.

"Kamla, this is Kate Perry at River's Edge, and it's about ten o'clock, recess time, and for once I don't have yard duty. Anyhow, I'm sorry you're sick. There's a lot of that flu around. Get lots of rest, which I assume you're doing with your answering machine on. Kamla, the reason I called, besides saying I'm sorry you're sick, is that I can't find the song sheets and posters for your Open House skit tonight. Will you give me a call at the school and let me know where to look? Just leave a message in the office. Thanks. 'Bye."

Nancy stared at the machine. "The last call came in at ten o'clock this morning. Hmmm. Wonder when the first one came in." She held down the Rewind button until the tape was back at the beginning. Then she hit Play. There was a long buzz and then a dial tone.

"A hang-up," she muttered. "I hate it when people do that."

"Probably some automated sales pitch," George said. "I still can't figure out how one machine knows it's talking to another machine!"

The next call was definitely not a sales pitch. Nancy held up her hand to shush George and turned up the volume. They stood and stared at each other as a melodic voice filled the room.

"Kamla! This is Jodi. I'm so excited, I can hardly wait. It's all falling into place so neatly. Looks like I'll be seeing you soon! Give Jeremy a kiss for me and a hug for yourself. I'm turning in. Sorry I missed you! I'll be in touch."

Chapter

Ten

Nancy sat down in the desk chair with a thump, feeling as if someone had punched her in the stomach. "That'll cinch Sam's suspicions about Kamla," she said.

George nodded. "Can't we erase it?" she asked, glaring at the machine as if it were a hostile alien. Then, before Nancy could answer, she quickly said, "No, strike that! I wouldn't tamper with evidence. But I would like to know what the message means. What do you make of it, Nan?"

"I don't know, but I plan to find out," Nancy replied. "If the school call was made this morning at ten, then Jodi's call probably came in last night."

"And she said she was going to turn in . . ."

"I think we need to talk to Jodi Fontaine,"

Nancy said as she opened the middle drawer of Kamla's desk and rummaged around for a personal phone directory. "Kamla said she had Jodi's private number. I just hope she's written it down somewhere."

George was going through the three side drawers of the desk while Nancy was talking.

"This may be it!" she said excitedly as she pulled a well-used address book from the top drawer. She turned to the Fs. "Yup, here we are, Jodi Fontaine. I hope she's calling in for her messages while she's in Mexico."

Nancy took the book and punched in the numbers. "It's ringing," she said to George, expectantly. The expression on her face changed. "A recording," she explained.

George paced up and down the living room of the apartment while Nancy completed the call. When she hung up, Nancy swiveled around in the chair. "Well, her recording says she'll return the call. I left my name and home number."

"And now?" George asked.

"Now I roll the answering machine tape ahead to where it was, and we get out of here before Sam's investigators arrive and start asking us questions!"

"What was the other call?"

"Just another hang-up."

The girls turned out the light and locked the door behind them. When they had barely reached the car, a green sedan pulled up in front of the building. Two men got out and climbed the stairs to the second story.

"Nobody home, fellas," Nancy said under her breath as she drove off.

Two blocks away from the apartment, she pulled into a gas station.

"What now?" George asked.

"I want to call Wright," Nancy said. "Find out if anyone has made contact with him. And then we'll go over to the police station and see if Sam has come up with anything more."

A strong wind was blowing when Nancy got out of the car, and overhead the sky looked heavy and black. She shivered and thought about Jeremy, hoping that whoever had him had taken him to a warm and sheltered place. If Kamla had him, at least he would be well taken care of. She pushed the thought aside. Kamla was not a kidnapper! But that message from Jodi was strange. Maybe they *were* working together.

She dropped the coins in the slot and punched in Edwin Wright's number. One ring, two, and on the third ring she heard a muted click. The police recorder was operating.

"Edwin Wright," he said.

"Mr. Wright, this is Nancy Drew. I'm just checking to see if you've heard anything more."

"Yes, we've had a call," he said. He sounded like he enjoyed giving Nancy the information. "A person with a foreign accent called—a woman—

muffling her voice, of course. It's all on the tape. I have an officer here with me."

"Well, what did she say?" Nancy asked, ignoring his veiled reference to Kamla.

"Only that further instructions would be forthcoming, and that Jeremy was safe."

"Did you actually talk to Jeremy?"

There was a pause. "No."

"Mr. Wright," Nancy said. "It would really help to have more information on Jack Farmer. Is there any way you can get someone to find that file tonight?"

"The police are working on the case, Ms. Drew. I really don't see any necessity . . ."

Nancy took a deep breath and looked skyward. "Forgive me, Sam," she muttered at the heavens. She could just see Sam's reaction when he heard this on the tape.

"Excuse me?" Wright said.

"I'm at the police station," Nancy fibbed, "and we need more on the Farmer case. Tonight! Request of Officer Sam Fanelli!"

"Oh," Wright said. "Well, in that case, I'll see if I can get my law clerk to find it."

"Good," said Nancy quickly. "I'll be by in an hour to pick it up—and bring it back to the station."

When she slid back behind the wheel, Nancy's expression was pensive.

"Well, what happened?" George asked.

"They've had one call," Nancy replied, shivering. "Brrr! I think we're in for some cold weather. Wright thinks it's Kamla. He said the caller had a foreign accent. They've got the caller's voice on tape."

"L it is Kamla, a voiceprint will identify her," George said, almost to herself.

"Yes," Nancy said, "and it wouldn't be hard to pick up a control tape. She recorded her own message on her answering machine, and I'll bet there are classroom tapes at the school that she recorded. They're waiting for another call now."

"And what do you think?"

"Well, it's possible that Jodi and Kamla are working together. But I think that Farmer is still our most likely lead, and that if that caller was Kamla, she was forced to make the call. Right now they need to concentrate on finding Farmer, and Sam can't do that without all the information." Nancy shoved the key in the ignition and started the engine with a roar. "So I told Wright that I was at the police station, and that Detective Fanelli wanted his file on Farmer, and that I would pick it up from his house in an hour. He's calling Shelley Lawson to go and find it."

"Is this a confession?" George asked, a grin spreading across her face.

"Well, it was a fib," Nancy admitted. "But if the police won't concentrate on Jack Farmer, I will! I think Jeremy's life depends on finding that man. And it's not going to be a great night for a search." As she spoke, big raindrops began to splash down, a few at first, and then more, until suddenly, with a crash of thunder, the sky opened up and sheets of cold, driving rain pounded on the pavement.

The parking lot at the police station was full, and every light in the building was on. Nancy parked on a side street, and the two girls dashed to the front entrance. Three uniformed officers were talking to the duty officer and, looking down the hall toward the conference rooms, Nancy could see several plainclothes officers hurrying in and out.

"What's going on?" she asked the duty officer. "I've never seen this place so busy at this time of night."

The young man at the desk nodded. "Haven't you had your radio on?" Then, without waiting for an answer, he continued. "This storm took out a levee and a power station upriver, and we're getting ready to evacuate two nursing homes. No heat, no lights, but lots of water. We're supposed to get freezing rain here, too. A major cold front coming through from Canada." He craned his neck for a look through the glass windows in the door. "Looks like we're getting it now," he said. "If that isn't enough, we have a family disturbance over on Twenty-fourth Street, and an APB out on a kidnapper. You name it, lady, and tonight, we've got it. Now, how can I help you?"

"I'd like to talk to Sam Fanelli," Nancy said. "If that's possible."

"He just got through with the captain," the officer said. "Let me ring his desk. What's your name, please?"

Nancy and George stood at the front counter while the officer located Sam and gave him the message. A few minutes later Sam came to the end of the hallway to greet them, and Nancy felt some of her tension draining away.

"Come on back," he said, "I have some more information for you." He ushered them into the same small conference room they had been in the night before. "Have a seat. I'll get the file and be right back."

"I hope his information isn't about Kamla," George said. "I don't need any more bad news tonight. And I know those policemen going up to her apartment were going to listen to that taped message from Jodi."

"Right," Nancy agreed. She was about to say something else, when Sam came back into the room with a sheet of paper. "This was faxed to us tonight by the FBI," he said. "Apparently, this guy Farmer worked across state lines and got himself in trouble with a number of agencies. Anyhow, the piece that I didn't have earlier was that in his last job, he had a female accomplice. Her birth name is Nora Smith, but she hasn't used that since she was fifteen—she changes names like other people change clothes. The Feds think that she was the brains behind his extortion racket. She was never caught, and she's very good at disguises. She walked away—he got sent up for three years. Nice lady!"

"Description?" Nancy asked.

"Nothing definitive," said Sam, "except her height, five eight. She changes her hair color, her eyes—with tinted contact lenses, her skin color with makeup—even her body shape and weight with padding."

"Well, thanks," Nancy said, standing up.

"Give me the keys," George said. "I'll get the car."

As she closed the door firmly behind her, Sam put his arm loosely around Nancy's shoulders. Her cheeks flushed, and goose bumps ran up and down her arms. She looked up into Sam's eyes and then dropped her glance.

"Nan, I did put out an APB on your friend Kamla Chadi. I have to take Edwin Wright's suspicions seriously." He took her chin in his hand and turned her head, forcing her to look at him. "But I also put out an APB on Farmer, based on what you told me. He's also a prime suspect, and I'll let you know when we pick him up."

"Thanks, Sam—" Nancy started to say, but the words were lost as he pulled her close.

Footsteps sounded in the hall, and Sam released Nancy just as the door burst open and an older man came in.

"Sam!" he said. "You know that Jack Farmer you were looking for?"

Sam nodded. "What about him, John?"

The officer looked at Nancy questioningly.

"It's okay," Sam said. "This is my friend Nancy Drew. She's a private investigator. In fact, she's working on that case. Nancy, meet Officer John Spanos."

Nancy smiled and extended her hand.

"Pleased to meet you, Ms. Drew. Well, about Farmer. We got a call from a construction crew foreman an hour ago. He'd gone back to the site on the north edge of town to secure their equipment, what with the storm and all, and he stumbled on this body in the ditch."

Nancy gripped the back of the chair tightly. She could anticipate what John Spanos was going to say, and her fear for Jeremy welled up.

"The foreman called for an ambulance, but the guy was DOA. They took the body to the morgue. Coroner just called here with an ID on him. It was Jack Farmer, alias Arnie Beyers."

Chapter

Eleven

Any sign of the boy?" Sam asked.

"No, nothing. The only piece of evidence we picked up was the murder weapon," Officer Spanos said.

"Which was . . ." Sam prompted him.

"Which was a silver-handled knife—almost a stiletto, with a very ornate handle, all carved. Looked to me like it was Pakistani or Indian." He nodded his head knowingly at Sam. "Seems like sending the fellows over to talk to the kid's teacher was a good idea. I had the dispatcher radio them to bring her in."

Nancy's hand was still locked in a tight grip on the back of the chair, and her mind was whirling. Jack Farmer was dead, murdered with a knife like one she had seen in Kamla's apartment. There was no sign of Jeremy. Kamla was missing, and the police were looking for her. Jodi had left that strange message on the answering machine, and Edwin Wright, who had started the whole thing, was at home recording calls from ransom seekers!

"Thanks, John," Sam said as the other man left the room. He put his hands on Nancy's shoulders and turned her around to face him.

"Nan, believe me, we're doing our best to find Jeremy and to find out who took him."

"Sam! Listen to me. Kamla is not a criminal!" Nancy said, pushing away.

"I am listening to you," Sam protested. Gently, he rested his hand on her arm. "Now you listen to me. At the moment all the evidence we have points to Kamla and the boy's mother. We have the physical evidence—the bracelet, the threatening calls to Edwin Wright, and now possibly the murder weapon, which sounds like it may have come from her place. And in addition, we found a message from Jodi Fontaine on Kamla Chadi's answering machine that said 'It's all falling into place, and I'll be seeing you soon.' Does that sound like they're working together or not?"

Nancy dropped her voice. "I know it sounds bad and looks bad, but I think Farmer talked to somebody about Wright's scheme and got double-crossed."

"You may be right," he said. "We're checking it out."

"Oh, Sam, I'll be glad when this is over. I don't like being your adversary."

Sam gave her a warm smile. "That's why we have to keep our personal and professional lives separate." He paused. "How about dinner Saturday night if I'm not working? Just Sam and Nan, not Detective Sam and Nancy, PI. Some place with soft lights and good food and . . ."

"I'd like that," Nancy murmured.

"I'll call you," he said.

When Nancy got outside, the rain had turned to sleet and it was bitterly cold. She pulled her jacket tightly around her. George was parked at the curb, feigning sleep.

"Oh," she said, yawning, "is the party over, or is this just intermission?"

"You goof," Nancy said, punching her arm, "I've got a lot of things to tell you, none of them very good."

As they drove along the dark, slippery streets, heading for the Wright estate, Nancy summarized for George what she had learned in the police station.

"So the file on Farmer isn't going to do us much good at this point," George said. "He's now out of the picture, and Jeremy is still missing."

"Hard to tell. There may be some clue in there that will lead us to an accomplice."

"The mysterious Nora."

"Yes. My hunch is that Farmer told somebody

about Wright's scheme to 'kidnap' Jeremy and got double-crossed. So knowing more about Farmer might still help us."

A low-slung white sports car was parked in front of the mansion, and George parked the Mustang behind it.

"Not a bad piece of machinery," she said enviously. "That would cost a chunk of cash. It can't belong to the cop that's here."

"No," Nancy said. She pointed to a beat-up two-door vehicle parked farther down the driveway. "I'll bet *that* one is the cop's."

Edwin Wright responded to their ring and showed them into his study. A boxlike reel-to-reel tape recorder was on the desk beside the phone, and an officer was sitting in an easy chair beside the desk.

Edwin Wright made the introductions. "Ms. Drew, Ms. Fayne . . . Officer Whiteall." He turned to face Shelley Lawson, who was perched on the arm of another chair. "And I believe you have both met my law clerk, Shelley Lawson. She tells me that you were in to see me today while I was in court." The disapproval in his voice was evident.

Shelley was elegantly dressed in a slim, emerald green silk sheath. Her fabric high-heeled pumps were dyed to match, and she wore diamond stud earrings and a matching diamond brooch, pinned strategically at the revealing V-neckline of her dress. Obviously, the call to come to Edwin Wright's with the file had interrupted her other plans.

Nancy and George acknowledged the woman, who ignored Wright's disparaging tone and beamed at them like old friends. "I didn't think I'd be seeing you again so soon," she said. "This kidnapping has been a terrible strain on Mr. Wright. I think he's bearing up remarkably well under difficult circumstances."

"Have you heard anything more?" Nancy asked.

Officer Whiteall looked up. "No," he said, but even as he spoke, the phone rang. Tension filled the room, as if everyone had stopped breathing. Once. Twice. On the third ring, Wright picked up the receiver. Whiteall adjusted the speaker on the recorder.

"Edwin Wright here."

"Edwin, this is Jodi Fontaine. I'd like to speak to Jeremy, please."

Wright hesitated briefly. "You can't!—I mean, he's sleeping. Don't you know what time it is?"

Jodi's response was restrained. "I'm sorry if I'm calling too late," she said. "Do we have a bad line? I keep hearing an echo."

Whiteall quickly reached over and adjusted the volume down. The room was silent as they all strained to hear.

"Edwin," Jodi continued, "it's imperative that I speak with Jeremy. Now!"

THE NANCY DREW FILES

"I need you to get off the line. I'm expecting an important call," Wright replied.

"*This* is an important call! Where is Jeremy?" Restraint was no longer a factor. Jodi Fontaine was agitated, and her terse demand informed everyone listening that she knew something was wrong.

Without a word, a flustered Edwin Wright handed the receiver to Nancy.

"Ms. Fontaine, this is Nancy Drew."

"Nancy Drew! You left a message for me. I've been trying to reach you—and Kamla—and all I get are answering machines at both numbers. What's going on? Where is Jeremy?"

Nancy took a deep breath. "Ms. Fontaine . . . Jodi . . ."

"He *has* been kidnapped, hasn't he? It's true! It wasn't a ruse!"

"The police are working on it. There's an officer here now."

Jodi Fontaine started to cry. A shiver ran up Nancy's neck. Was this Jodi Fontaine, the actress? Jodi Fontaine, in cahoots with Kamla to wrest Jeremy away from Edwin Wright? Or was this Jodi, the mother? "Why do you think he's been kidnapped?" Nancy asked.

Jodi was trying to control her sobbing. "Because . . . because I've received a demand for ransom money. Nobody even told me my son was missing! Why didn't his grandfather call me?"

"Who demanded money?" Nancy asked.

"I don't know! A man. He said he had Jeremy."

As Nancy spoke, George positioned herself to watch Edwin Wright's reaction. Shelley Lawson had moved over behind the chair he was sitting in and was patting his shoulder solicitously. The scent of her expensive perfume filled the room.

"I don't know who it was!" Jodi continued. "I was told to transfer funds to a bank somewhere in the Caribbean. All I was given was the account number."

"Before you do—" Nancy started to say.

"Ms. Drew, my son's life is at stake!" Jodi yelled. "My accountant has already sent the money—half a million dollars. I'm leaving right now for River Heights. I'll be there tomorrow."

Jodi Fontaine hung up without saying goodbye, and the impersonal dial tone hummed through the room.

"I hope you don't believe that folderol," Wright said angrily. "How do we know she sent half a million dollars anywhere? How do we know she's not in cahoots with that . . . that foreign teacher and trying to put up a smoke screen until they get Jeremy out of the country?"

Nancy replaced the receiver and looked at him. "We don't know anything for sure, Mr. Wright, but I'm inclined to believe her. May I see the information on Jack Farmer?" she asked.

He nodded toward the desk, and she picked up the file and thumbed through the pages.

"I thought Detective Fanelli wanted the file," Wright said suspiciously.

"True," Nancy said, thinking fast. "But I just saw him at the police station, and I told him I'd look through the file myself and relay anything pertinent."

"Do they have any further developments in the case?" Shelley asked. She was sitting on the arm of a leather chair, daintily swinging a pretty leg, a green pump dangling from her toes.

"No," Nancy fibbed, deciding that information of the discovery of Farmer's body had been given to her in confidence, and it was Sam's place to inform Wright of the murder. She turned some pages in the file and looked over at Wright. "It seems that some pages are missing," she said, frowning. "It skips from page twenty-two to page thirty-one. Do you know where they are?"

"I have no idea," Wright answered. "Shelley?"

Shelley shrugged prettily. "We've had a terrible time with file clerks in the office," she explained. "One of the vocational schools called and asked if we would hire some of their students . . . and . . . well, remembering what it was like to be a struggling student, I went along with it. I hired two people to do filing, and I swear, neither one of them knew the alphabet! My guess is that pages twenty-three through thirty are stuck in somebody else's file, where they'll never be found again."

She picked up her coat from the back of the chair and moved toward the door. "Well, I'm sorry I have to leave," she said. "I have a date waiting for me at the Olympia Room. It's the annual St. Patrick's Day dinner and dance to benefit the homeless." She glanced at her jeweled wristwatch and patted Edwin Wright's arm once more. "Try to get some rest. I'll see you in the morning." Her voice was syrupy. "I do hope this all works out with a happy ending, and that little Jeremy is returned safe."

She closed the door softly behind her, but the scent of her perfume lingered in the room. The powerful roar from the engine of her sports car announced her final departure.

"Best law clerk I ever had," Wright said, admiringly. "She is so bright and knows as much about criminal law as any attorney. She's my right hand in the office."

"How long has she been with you?" Nancy asked.

"Oh, about three years. She came with wonderful references."

"You must pay her well," George said innocently, "considering the way she dresses and the car she drives."

"Of course!" Wright responded. "I pay all my employees well. But Shelley doesn't have to work. She *chooses* to. She got an inheritance from her parents' estate just before she came to River Heights. She's a very independent young woman."

Nancy tossed George her jacket. "Well, I think we'll be leaving now," she said to Wright. "Thank you for letting me see the file on Farmer."

She practically pushed George through the front door and walked swiftly to the Mustang. "Let's go!" she said, turning the key in the ignition.

"Where are we going? And what was in that file?" George asked.

"What was missing was almost as important as what was there. As far as I could figure, the pages that had been taken out dealt with Farmer's accomplice—the woman named Nora Smith. But they forgot to take out one very important reference to her. She was born in Shelley, Oklahoma!"

Chapter

Twelve

GEORGE LET OUT a low whistle. "I guess I don't have to ask where we're going now."

"Right, the Olympia Room, and I hope Shelley Lawson wasn't lying about going there."

George looked down at her jeans. "*She* was dressed for a dinner dance, we're not. That could be a problem."

"No problem," Nancy said. "I went to their St. Patrick's Day party last year, and people were wearing all kinds of outfits, from dressy to really casual. It's a benefit, there's no dress code, and they're not going to turn anybody away. Especially in this weather." Nancy reached over and turned up the car heater. "It's going to hurt the attendance."

The Olympia Room was a trendy restaurant on the top floor of a new high-rise office building. At lunchtime, it was filled with office workers, and at night it was often rented out for private parties.

When Nancy entered the multilevel parking structure adjacent to the building, there were a few scattered empty spaces available.

"I think I'll cruise through here first," Nancy said, "and see if I can spot her car before we go upstairs."

"Do you think that Shelley and Wright were working together on this?" George asked. "Like Wright and Farmer were?"

"No, I have a hunch that Farmer talked to Shelley about Wright's plan, and she figured she could cash in on it. But that's a guess. And unfortunately, the evidence right now points to Kamla, which means Jodi could be involved, too."

"Shelley's here, all right!" George interrupted excitedly. "There's her car."

Nancy slowed for a look at the white sports car, cruised past it, and then suddenly hit the brakes.

"Whoa!" George yelled, grabbing the dashboard in surprise. She looked at Nancy questioningly.

"Look to the left," Nancy whispered in a tone of disbelief. "That's Kamla's car."

"I don't get it," said George.

"Neither do I," Nancy replied.

Still puzzled by finding their friend's car in the parking lot, they took the elevator up to the restaurant and were greeted by a man dressed in bright green pants and vest, wearing a green felt hat with a long feather shooting skyward from under a black band. "And it's a fine-looking pair of colleens we have here! Sure an' begorra! It's you I adorra!" he said as they paid their admission.

"I bet you say that to everybody," George teased. "Did you happen to see a pretty blond woman dressed in green come in?"

The man laughed. "At least fifty of them," he said.

"What about a young Indian woman in a sari?" Nancy asked.

"I'm *sari!*" The man laughed. "Get it? Sorry? Sari? But no, seriously, that's one I would have noticed. Have a good time, girls! The bar is on your left if you want sodas. The buffet's on the right, and the dance floor is straight ahead."

They thanked him and pushed their way into the room, which was decorated with shamrocks, green streamers, and posters of leprechauns.

"Can we eat first?" George asked pleadingly.

"Not a chance," Nancy answered. "We need to find Shelley and see who she's with, which won't be easy in this mob."

A live band was playing, and the dance floor across the room was crowded. They pushed their way through the maze of tables in the dining area, studying groups of people as they went, looking for Kamla and Shelley.

"Georgie!" A man's voice called out over the raucous music and George turned quickly. A tall, husky young man wearing a cowboy hat stood up at one of the tables and beamed at her. Nancy recognized him as a fellow George had once dated for about six months. "Come join us, Georgie," he said, motioning her toward a table crowded with partyers.

"Hi, Duke!" George said. "Good to see you again! I can't right now! Maybe a little bit later, but thanks for the invitation."

Nancy, with George following, moved determinedly to the edge of the dance floor, where a slightly tipsy man whom George didn't recognize reached out and caught Nancy by the arm.

"Just one little dance," the man said to Nancy. "You're the prettiest girl in the room!" He held her arm possessively, and Nancy smiled as she extricated herself from his grip.

"Thank you," she said, raising an eyebrow at George and pointing. "But my boyfriend's over there watching, and I have to join him."

George picked up the signal. Nancy was pointing across the dance floor toward an exit sign. She craned her neck. Shelley Lawson was standing by the door, talking to a man in a suit. Shelley looked up, frowned slightly as she spotted Nancy and George, and spoke again to the man. He looked at them across the dance floor, then opened the door. As he and Shelley left the room,

Nancy noticed Shelley exchanging glances with the tipsy man on her right.

"Let's go, George," said Nancy. "Hurry! We'll lose them!"

Surprised and annoyed glances followed the young women as they elbowed through the dancers to the door on the other side. The hallway on the east side of the building led to a bank of elevators. The doors were closing on Shelley and the man just as Nancy and George got there. Nancy jabbed at the Call button for another elevator, eyeing the screen above the car Shelley was on. "We're on the tenth floor," she murmured.

George was also watching. The marker stopped. "She's going down to the fourth."

"I'm not so sure," Nancy countered quietly. Several other people had left the party and were waiting. "She won't want us to know where she's going. She'll get off at four and either walk down to three or walk up one floor to five. One flight of stairs is about all she can manage in those heels! Did you see Kamla anywhere in that room?"

"No, not a sign," George said. "But I did just click in on that guy in the suit talking to Shelley. I thought he looked familiar."

"Who was he?" Nancy asked.

"Remember in the law building garage today when we saw Farmer driving one of Uncle Joe's green-and-yellow trucks?"

"Yes."

"Well," George said, "he was the man in the passenger seat."

An elevator stopped, the doors opened, and the people filed in. Most were going to the main floor, but one pretty young office worker announced that she had to go back and clean off her desk. She pushed the sixth-floor button.

Nancy glanced at George. "I'm going to five," she said. George picked up the cue, leaned forward, and pushed the buttons for both five and three. If Nancy was going to five, that meant she was going to three.

Just as the doors were closing, the man who had been pestering Nancy for a dance came rushing at the elevator. "Hold it!" he yelled.

Another man amiably held the doors open until the pesky guy could enter. He looked at the people around him, not acknowledging that he had spoken to Nancy earlier, and he seemed much less tipsy now than he had at the dance. Nancy recalled the look he'd exchanged with Shelley, and a warning flag waved in her head.

The elevator descended slowly, stopping at six to let off the office worker. At the next floor Nancy was ready. She waited a few seconds after the doors opened fully, before she made a move. When they were about to close again, she stepped out onto the fifth floor. But right behind her, she heard the man saying, "Excuse me, folks. This is my floor. Almost missed it!"

"Mine, too!" Nancy heard George's voice, but her request came too late. The doors closed and the elevator rumbled down to the fourth floor. Nancy walked briskly down the long hall, aware that the man was following. Black-edged gold lettering on glass door windows announced the names of some of the businesses; others had solid wood doors with nameplates attached. Many were real estate firms and insurance companies.

Nancy looked for a trace of light showing through the glass or under the doors of the offices as she hurried by. But she saw none. Behind which door was Shelley Lawson hiding? Somewhere to her left she heard the hum of a vacuum cleaner. At least there was someone else on the fifth floor besides her and her pursuer. And she knew that George had sensed the danger and would be getting off at the floor below and taking the stairs back up, probably two at a time.

The carpeting in the hallway muffled footsteps, and Nancy resisted the urge to turn around to see where the man was. Maybe it was coincidence that he had asked her to dance, but she didn't think so. And had Shelley's glance across the dance floor been at Nancy and George, or at the supposedly tipsy reveler? Was he a cohort? Was Jeremy being held in one of these offices? And where was Kamla?

There was no place for Nancy to hide. She quickened her pace, half jogging. The building was like a maze with intersecting shorter hallways curving to the right and left off the main hall. But a quick look verified that these were dead ends. Up ahead, she could see a green Exit sign, and underneath that, Stairs.

She was approaching the exit when, up ahead of her, the double doors to a large office opened, and a custodian came out pushing a cleaning cart. Brooms, mops, a dustpan, and other cleaning paraphernalia stuck out from the sides of the cart, which had a large bin in the center for trash. He was whistling.

"Wait!" Nancy called.

The custodian waved at her and continued along the hall, turning right at the next corridor.

Surely George would be coming up those stairs and through the door any moment. A sudden thought occurred to Nancy. Maybe the man following her worked in one of these offices. Maybe he was a real estate broker. Or an insurance salesman. Maybe he didn't have any connection with Shelley Lawson at all. Maybe this was just her overactive imagination. But then why was he suddenly so quick and alert, so different from the way he'd been at the party? Enough guessing. Nancy stopped and very deliberately turned around and looked behind her. The man was gone! He was nowhere in sight!

Feeling like an utter fool, she swirled back around, letting out a sigh of relief. But her relief was short-lived. She sensed, rather than heard, someone breathing behind her. He must have ducked into one of the intersecting hallways when she looked behind her! Before she could turn, the man spoke.

"We are going into that office across the hall, Ms. Drew," he said, firmly gripping her arm. Though it was the same man from the dance upstairs, his voice was cold sober now. "Don't make any noise, and don't resist me. What you feel pressing into your back is a revolver with a silencer, and I won't hesitate to use it."

Chapter

Thirteen

NANCY DID EXACTLY as she was told. She knew better than to argue with a gun. The man steered her toward the massive double doors of the office that the custodian had left just minutes before.

"Open the door," he said brusquely.

Nancy reached for the brass knob. A sign on the door said Office for Rent and listed a phone number. Before she pushed the door open, Nancy's eyes darted to the right for one last look down the hall. She was certain that she had seen a shadow just at the time the man stuck the gun in her back. It had to be George coming from the stairwell. She must have ducked into an alcove. Good! George would call Sam, and Sam would get here in a hurry.

She opened the door, and the man pushed her

into the room. Shelley Lawson and the man in
the suit—the same man George had seen in the
TV repair shop truck—were standing by the
window, arguing heatedly. A nighttime pan-
orama of River Heights spread out below, with
the usually sparkling lights of the city blurred by
the driving sleet that was hitting the window.
There were two desks in the room and several easy chairs. It looked like a reception
office for a prosperous firm.

Shelley swung around to face them when the
door closed. "There were *two* of them!" she
yelled at the man who had brought Nancy in.
"Where's the other one?" Without waiting for an
answer, she turned to the man beside her and
snapped, "Go get the other one, Frank!"

Nancy closed her eyes, hoping that George had
immediately gone to call Sam. But deep down,
she knew better. She knew that if she had been in
George's shoes, she would have investigated the
office Nancy was forced into before leaving. So
when Frank yanked open the door, she wasn't
surprised to see George crouched there, trying to
hear the conversation inside.

"Surprise!" Frank said as George toppled into
the room. He reached down and grabbed her
arm, jerking her to her feet, and kicked the door
shut. "Here's number two, Madam CEO," he
said to Shelley, in a pronounced British accent
and with a strong overtone of sarcasm. "And are

115

we going to give these two a smashing train ride as well—or do you have other plans?" He waved a hand in a grand gesture at Shelley. "I could summon Ken to come back with an oversize custodial cart, but that's just a suggestion, you understand. I wouldn't want to interfere with your grand plan."

"Watch your mouth, Frank," Shelley said. "If you don't like the way I do things, then you can move on and form your own consulting group."

"I may just do that," he replied tersely.

Shelley opened a briefcase on one of the desks and smiled across the room at Nancy and George, who were both being watched by the man with the gun. "Girl detectives," she said, shaking her head as a mother would at naughty children. "You get yourselves into so much trouble. Although I must say you're brighter than most adult detectives I've run into." From the briefcase she took a small bottle of colorless liquid and two slim paper-wrapped packages that turned out to be hypodermic needles. "This will calm you down for a few hours while we conclude our project."

"Shelley," Nancy said, "quit while you're ahead. The police are onto you," she fibbed. "It's only a matter of minutes before they get here." She took a wild stab at a possibility. "They know you had Farmer killed—"

"Take off her jacket and hold her!" Shelley

ordered, nodding at George and ignoring Nancy's monologue.

Frank and the other man slipped George's arms out of her jacket and held her.

"This won't hurt at all," Shelley said, deftly sticking the needle into George's arm. Instantly, George slumped over and, while Nancy watched horrified, the men dragged George over to one of the armchairs.

"You're next," Shelley said as she prepared a new syringe. She looked over at Frank. "When we've finished our other job, you come back for them with the van. Bert can help you load them."

It was the last thing Nancy heard before she lapsed into unconsciousness.

When she came to, her head was throbbing and her eyes wouldn't focus properly. She was lying on the floor by the desk. Her feet had been bound with tape and her hands taped behind her back. Muted ceiling lights gave the illusion of dusk. To her right she could hear George moaning.

"George," Nancy whispered. Her mouth was dry and her throat was sore. "George!"

There was a groan followed by a dry cough. "I'm over here," George said. Her voice was raspy and her speech was slurred. "In the chair."

"Did they tape your hands and feet?"

"I dunno." There were shuffling sounds from the chair. Nancy could tell that George was making an effort to clear her head and concentrate on her hands and feet. "Yes, I'm taped," George answered. "Where are you?"

"On the floor by the desk. I'm going to roll toward you. We've got to get out of here before they come back for us."

"How're we gonna do that?" George asked sleepily, struggling to keep awake. "Not possible."

"It is *too* possible!" Nancy said sharply. "You're going to untape me, and I'm going to untape you." With a few gentle thumps, Nancy rolled across the floor toward George. "Feet first," she announced.

Sitting on the floor at George's feet, with her back to George's legs, Nancy started picking at the tape around George's ankles. She worked slowly and clumsily, hampered by her own bound wrists, yet knowing that haste would not help.

"Okay, hands next," she said to George, when she had stripped the last piece of tape from around her ankles.

"Out of my way! I may fall over when I stand up," said George, who was becoming more clear-headed. Nancy rolled out of the way, and George stood up on shaky legs. "Maybe we can work on each other's wrists."

"I think one at a time," Nancy said. "Squat down here by me so I can get started. It's going to be slow, and they're going to be back soon."

"Hang on a minute," George said. "I can see a drawer partially open in that desk. Maybe I can find a paper knife or something to give us a hand."

She walked to the desk, backed up to the drawer, and pulled it open. Then she turned around and surveyed the contents.

"Better than a paper knife! Nail scissors! Oh, I'm glad somebody left these babies behind." She turned her back to the drawer again and looped her little finger into the handle of the scissors. "Got 'em!"

Walking to where Nancy was sitting, George sat on the floor so they were back-to-back. "Okay," she said, "I can't see what I'm doing, Nan, so you'll have to yell if I cut skin instead of tape."

"Count on it," Nancy said, laughing.

It didn't take long for George to cut Nancy's tape, and shortly after, her own wrists and Nancy's ankles were also free.

"Let's get out of here," George said, "before those slimeballs come back."

"Wait a minute. I want to check out these desks first. It looks like they just helped themselves to a vacant office. They probably got a key from somebody in the building, or picked a lock. But maybe Shelley and her goons left something behind." She walked over to the larger of the two desks and pulled open a drawer. "Three paper clips," she reported dejectedly.

"Nan, I think I've got something over here!" George's voice was excited. "Someone was using this phone, and they forgot to take their notes with them."

"What does it say?" Nancy reached for the pad and together, the two girls puzzled over the notations. Someone had scribbled "Brady," a phone number, and, below it, what appeared to be 12:32.

"Who's Brady?" George asked.

Nancy shook her head. "I don't know. It's a local number. Only one way to find out." She picked up the receiver and punched in the numbers.

George walked over to the window and stared out into the darkness. The storm had not abated. "We've got to get out of here," she said, looking nervously at her watch.

"Just a minute, it's ringing," Nancy said. "Let me see who answers."

"Midwest Railroad," an official voice announced into Nancy's ear.

Surprised at reaching a business, Nancy recovered quickly. "Good evening," she said, as if she had all the time in the world. "Mr. Brady?"

"Who?"

"Mr. Brady . . . or maybe Ms. Brady . . . ?"

"Sorry, lady, no Brady working here."

"Oh." Disappointed, Nancy had to think fast. This was the only clue they had. Maybe if she kept the man on the line, she could find out why the railroad number was on that notepad. Something!

"Well, could you tell me when your next train comes in from . . . Chicago?" She bent down and picked up something from under the desk and stuffed it into the pocket of her jeans.

"Yup, that run comes in at ten-twenty tomorrow morning."

"Thanks," Nancy said. "I have to meet some friends . . . didn't want to be late . . ."

There was a brief pause, and the man cleared his throat. "Excuse me, miss, that's a freight train. Don't think your friends would be on that one. Midwest isn't running any passenger lines anymore. You'd have to call Central Railway for their schedule."

"Oh," Nancy said. She looked down at the paper again. "Do you have anything going through at twelve thirty-two?" she asked him, acting on a hunch.

"Oh, yes, sure do! That's what we call the Midnight Flyer, even though it's not really midnight. Showing it on time right now, but with this storm, might be a few minutes late." He paused. "You realize that this is a freight train, right?"

"Yes, I do," Nancy assured him, as she studied the note. "I was just curious. I have another question, if you don't mind."

"Ask away."

"Does *Brady* mean anything to you?"

"Well, no person here by that name," said the

man. "Only thing I can think of is the Brady Crossing. That's that bad one about ten miles east of town, where the old County Road Five intersects the tracks. The crossing's unmarked— no signal lights or arms or anything. We had a bad accident there four years ago. Fields all around it, nearest farmhouse is six miles. Usually not much traffic out there, 'specially late at night."

"Thank you very much," Nancy said. She hung up the receiver, stuffed the note in her pocket, and moved to the door. "Let's get out of here. We don't have much time."

"Where are we going?"

"To meet a freight train at Brady Crossing."

As she reached for the doorknob, the door swung open and Frank entered.

"What the—" he started to say, but he never finished. Nancy's right arm went up with a sharp karate motion and clipped him under the chin, and he fell to the floor in an unconscious heap.

"Nice one!" George said admiringly. "May we go now?"

"After you," Nancy said. She pushed Frank out of the way and closed the door firmly behind them. The two girls ran for the exit.

"Take the stairs!" Nancy said. "We don't want to meet up with the custodian."

"Do you think he was in on it?" George asked. "Shouldn't we look for him?"

"Don't have time now," Nancy replied, as they hurried to the parking lot.

"What's the rush? Do you think they had Jeremy hidden in that cart?"

"No," Nancy replied. She reached into her pocket and pulled out a red silk hair scarf. "This was on the floor under the desk. I think they had Kamla in the cart, and I think they plan to kill her!"

Chapter

Fourteen

"KILL KAMLA! Why?" George asked.

"They've set her up to be a suspect. The heat will be off them if she's killed while running away," Nancy said as they hurried into the parking garage. She stopped at a pay phone. "I need to call Wright and see if he's received any instructions. Got any change? My guess is that they'll pick up the money before that train goes through at 12:32 and be long gone before anyone connects them with Kamla's accident."

Silently, George handed her a quarter and walked down the aisle looking at the parked cars. Nancy could tell that she, too, was worried.

Nancy dialed and listened to the rings. On the third one the tape recorder clicked in. The recorder was still connected. Did that mean the kidnappers hadn't called? Was her theory wrong?

Or were the police being extra cautious? Maybe Jeremy had already been returned.

"Wright residence."

Hearing the familiar deep voice startled her.

"Sam!"

"Nancy! Where are you?"

"I'm in the Olympia parking garage, but I won't be here long. Have the kidnappers called with instructions yet?"

"About an hour ago," Sam reported. "They'll meet us at the dock of the Blue Water Ballroom, out on the River Road."

"That old deserted place?"

"Yup. I'm sure they think that if they're on water and we're on land, they'll have a better chance to escape. Besides, they know we won't do anything to endanger Jeremy."

"What time?" Nancy asked.

"Midnight. I'll be leaving here soon."

"Is Wright making the drop?" Nancy asked.

"No, they want his housekeeper to do it."

There was a short pause while Nancy did some thinking. She had met Wright's housekeeper that evening when she brought coffee into the den. The woman was five feet tall and sixty years old. There was no way Nancy could impersonate her. Besides, there wasn't enough time. It would be impossible to be on the River Road at midnight and at Brady Crossing at twelve-thirty.

"Nan, I know what you're thinking," Sam said. "Don't even consider it! It wouldn't work,

and I couldn't—I *wouldn't* let you take that risk.
I have a call in for one of our women officers.
She's a good match for Mrs. Henry in physical
size, and we can age her some with makeup.
She'll exchange the cash for Jeremy. They've
promised to have him at the drop site."

"Sam, did a man or a woman call?"

"A man, as far as we could make out. It was
muffled. Why?"

"Because I think Shelley Lawson, Wright's law
clerk, is Nora—the brains behind Jack Farmer's
last job. But she has men working with her. A
man named Frank, and somebody named Bert,
and a guy dressed as a custodian named Ken."

"Keep talking," Sam said, "I'm taking notes.
How do you know all this, Nan?"

"Because George and I just had a two-hour nap
at their insistence. Sam, the person who called—
did he let you talk to Jeremy?"

"Yes, the boy spoke to his grandfather. But just
a few sentences."

Nancy breathed a sigh of relief. "At least he's
still alive. And what about Kamla? Have you
found her?" she asked, hoping that Sam would
say the police had her safe in custody.

"Not yet," Sam replied. He sounded surprised
at the question. "We may pick her up at the drop
site. Frankly, at this point we're not sure who our
suspects are."

"You won't pick her up there," Nancy assured
him. "I'm sure Shelley Lawson has her. They're

going to set her up. Sam, there are two kidnap victims. And I think Shelley's planning an accident at Brady Crossing to kill Kamla!"

People were drifting back down to their cars from the party, and out of the corner of her eye, Nancy could see George leaning against the wall near the phone. A man wearing a leprechaun hat and green shoes lined up behind Nancy.

"Is she going to be all night on that thing?" Nancy heard him ask George, as he tapped his foot impatiently. "I need to make an important call."

"There are more phones on the next level," George told him, as she pointed up the ramp.

"My car is right over there," the man snapped. "I want to use *this* phone. I don't want to walk all the way up there when there's a perfectly good phone here."

Nancy covered her ear so she could hear Sam.

"Are you coming back here?" Sam asked Nancy.

"No. Sam, I'm heading for Brady Crossing. I think the gang is going to split up. Can you send a unit out there?"

"Nan, I'll do my best, but this weather is creating problems. We've got tie-ups on all major roads. Right now, every available car is assigned."

"Please try," Nancy said. "Or you could call the train dispatcher. They must have a two-way radio in the engine." She dropped her voice.

"Sam, Shelley Lawson's ruthless. And I think she's running this show. Be careful!"

"Hurry up, lady," said the leprechaun, eavesdropping on Nancy's conversation. "I have a ruthless girlfriend who's already furious because I'm late picking her up from work."

"Nan," Sam said, *"you* be careful. I'll try to get someone out there. And I'll try to get the dispatcher to radio the train. But the railroad may not agree to stop the train on a hunch." The frustration in his voice was obvious.

"Will you kiss him good-bye and get off that phone!" yelled the leprechaun.

"Thanks, Sam," Nancy said. " 'Bye."

"Well, it's about time!" the man said.

"If we weren't pushed for time, I'd stand right there and heckle him while he talks to his ruthless girlfriend," George muttered as they hurried toward Nancy's car. "Where to now?"

"Do you remember where Kamla's car was parked?" asked Nancy.

"Yeah, C-2 section, and I already looked while you were on the phone. It's gone. And so is Shelley's hot little number. Come to think of it, I wonder how Kamla got hers to run. She said she didn't have the five hundred to fix it."

"No, but it was worth a lot more than five hundred to our friends upstairs to get it running. If my hunch is right, somebody worked on that car or spent the cash to have it fixed."

George gave Nancy a quizzical look. "I'm not tracking," she said. "Explain."

"Look at it from Shelley's point of view," Nancy said. "If Kamla is running from the law, supposedly after kidnapping Jeremy, and her car, which is known for its bad behavior, stalls on the railroad tracks . . . and a train is coming . . ."

George shuddered. "So they had it fixed just so they could drive it to Brady Crossing, where it would be totaled with her in it. I can't believe anyone would be so heartless."

"They've already killed Farmer," Nancy reminded her, "probably so that Shelley could take over this scheme. And setting up Kamla will take the heat off them. Spending five hundred bucks to fix Kamla's car is no big deal when you're looking at collecting a million bucks—five hundred thousand each from Wright and Jodi. It's peanuts."

Another group from the party came streaming out of the elevator just as George and Nancy got into the Mustang.

"Georgie!" a man called out. "Georgie! Wait up a minute!" Heavy footsteps thudded on the concrete floor, and George's friend Duke squatted down by the passenger side so his face, crowned by his enormous cowboy hat, was framed in the window. "I never got my dance with you," he said, grinning. "Is that any way to treat a friend?"

"Sorry," George said. "Give me a call at home,

Duke. We're in a real big hurry." She glanced at her watch and turned to Nancy. "It's ten to twelve," she said.

"Big hurry?" Duke asked. "You got a heavy date or something?" His speech was slurred, and his eyes looked as if he'd had one beer too many.

"We've got a heavy date with a train," George said. "Move, Duke, so we can get out of here!"

"You don't want to hurry anywhere in this weather," he countered, leaning farther in through the window. "It's nasty out there. Freezing rain. Sleet. Who's your friend, Georgie? Why's she looking so mad?"

George rolled her eyes up to the ceiling. "Give me patience," she muttered. "Duke Avery, meet Nancy Drew." She unceremoniously pushed his elbow off the window frame and turned to Nancy.

"Good-bye, Duke. Let's go, Nan." Nancy didn't respond.

"Nan," George said quickly. "What's the matter?"

"This." Nancy turned the key in the ignition. Nothing happened. She tried it again. No response.

"Dead battery?" George wrinkled her forehead.

"Can't be—it's almost brand-new!" Nancy replied angrily. "We'll never make it to Brady Crossing! Not now!"

There was a polite cough from behind George. "Pleased to meet you, Nancy Drew," Duke said, his eyes sparkling mischievously. "Any friend of Georgie's is a friend of mine. And by the way, I'm a licensed mechanic. Why don't y'let me take a look under the hood? Could be something minor." Even while he was talking he was moving around to the front of the car.

"Thanks," Nancy said. "I appreciate the offer." Her frustration was apparent as she opened the door and got out. George climbed out of the passenger side and joined the two of them.

Duke was standing in front of the Mustang, hood up, shaking his head. "Can't believe this would happen in a high-class place like this," he said. He looked over at Nancy. "Almost new battery?" he repeated.

She nodded.

"No battery is more accurate," he said, pointing to the gaping hole where the battery should have been.

Chapter

Fifteen

Nancy pounded her fist on the fender. "That woman thinks of everything!" she said angrily. "I should have guessed that she'd mess up my car—just in case we escaped!"

Duke gave her a quizzical glance. "Escaped?"

"She knew exactly what to go for," George said, ignoring Duke's question. "She got a good look at your car in Wright's driveway. No question about who took it."

"You know a woman who steals batteries?" Duke said. "Man, oh man, now I've heard everything." He dropped the hood and snapped it into place. "Well, gals," he drawled, "looks like you're not going anywhere in this car." He took off his cowboy hat and waved it with a flourish in front of them, almost losing his balance with the gesture. "Oops! Duke's chauffeur service is at your service! Where would you like to go? The night is young. You want t'go look for this woman that stole your battery? I'd kind of like to get a look at her myself."

Nancy looked at her watch. It was a few minutes before midnight. "Duke," she said, "what we'd really like to do is borrow your car. We *need* to have a vehicle tonight—now!"

Duke looked at her with a half grin on his face. "Life and death situation, right?"

"That's exactly what it is," Nancy replied. "And we don't have much time. Where do you live?"

Duke pointed off to the north. "Oh, about ten minutes from here. But I don't have a car. Will a truck do?"

"Perfect!" Nancy said.

"So y'all are going to give me a ride home and take my truck, right?"

"Right, if you give me permission," Nancy replied with a grin.

Duke reached into his pockets and pulled out a key ring, dangling it in front of Nancy. "I'll give you permission if you promise me you'll keep it away from the Battery Lady," he said, stifling a yawn. "I'm ready for a nap. Tell you what. You can be my designated driver. I'll even give you permission to use my new cellular phone."

"Deal!" Nancy said, taking the keys and giving him a smile. "You may be saving someone's life. What's your address?"

"Number 2251 Lester Circle. My truck's parked right down here. It's that big white one." He lumbered off down the row with Nancy and George at his heels.

"What time is it?" Nancy asked George, when they got on the road. Duke's head was resting on George's shoulder, and he was snoring softly. Driving conditions were terrible. The streets were iced over, and the freezing rain had not abated. Nancy's impatience was evident.

"Twelve-ten," George said.

"Pray that the train will be late," Nancy said grimly, "or we'll never make it." She pulled into the driveway of Duke's house.

"Duke," George said, reaching across him and opening the passenger door. "Wake up. You're home. Thanks for the loan of your truck."

"You're welcome," he said groggily. "Bring it back in the morning."

"We will," George promised.

"With a battery," he added, wagging his finger at her.

"With a battery," George replied.

They were backing out of the driveway when Duke hurried off the porch, waving his arms.

"What now?" Nancy said, applying the brakes.

Duke, fully awakened by the weather, rushed up to the truck. "My house key is on that key ring," he said to Nancy.

She turned off the ignition and handed him the

keys. "Please hurry," she begged, feeling more and more frustrated.

A few minutes later George and Nancy were heading for County Road 5 and Brady Crossing. The windshield wipers beat an annoying rhythmic pulse that only smeared the frozen slush across the glass and reminded them of the passing minutes. They were out of the city now, and the gloomy flat fields stretched out on both sides, with deep ditches defining the roadway. Once, when Nancy touched the brake as a startled opossum scurried across the road, the truck went into a skid on the glazed surface. Expertly, she steered into the skid, then managed to pull the truck back on course without a major mishap.

"Nice recovery," George said, gripping the dashboard. "Let's see . . . if the train goes through town at twelve thirty-two, I figure it won't get to Brady Crossing until about twelve thirty-seven. If the storm has slowed it down, it might be twelve forty." She squinted at her watch in the light from the dashboard. "By my watch, we have about eight minutes till twelve thirty-seven. What's the plan?"

Nancy glanced over at her. "The terrain is so flat here, we'll be able to see the train coming from a few miles down. I figure that they'll park Kamla's car on the tracks . . ." She shuddered.

"With Kamla in it."

"Yes. Probably propped up in the driver's seat but unconscious."

"Nan." George paused, as if her thought was too terrible to voice. "Do you think that they've already killed her?"

Nancy shook her head. "No, forensic science is too good these days. The coroner could determine if she was dead before the train hit, and that would put Shelley and her friends back on the suspect list. They can't set up Kamla to be the kidnapper if she's already dead in her car." Nancy sighed. "I think Shelley will give her a shot, the same as she did with us, and probably cover for any traces of a sedative that the coroner might find in an autopsy by putting a bottle of pills in Kamla's purse. That way it will look like she took the drug voluntarily. And thanks to her henchman Frank, Shelley assumes that we're not around to blow her plans."

"Okay," George said, "here's what we'll do. You get as close to the track as you can without being on it, so I can jump out and pull Kamla from the driver's seat. Then—"

"No way!" Nancy protested. "I can't put you in jeopardy, too. I'll go for Kamla."

"Nan, use your head. We're talking seconds, not minutes. I can have my seat belt undone and my hand on the door handle before you even stop the truck. You can't do that. Just get me as close to the driver's side of Kamla's car as you can."

Nancy groaned and bit her lip. Tears glazed her

eyes as she looked over at George, with only the sound of the wipers and the wind interrupting the silence. Finally, Nancy spoke. "I should have had you drive," she said quietly.

"We're agreed, then? I get Kamla."

"Agreed. But, George, be careful. I . . . I don't want to . . ." Her voice choked. "I don't want to lose two friends."

"Nan, I promise you. I plan to be around to see Shelley Lawson in court."

Despite the seriousness of the situation, Nancy smiled. "Me, too. That will be one happy day," she said. "We're only a couple of miles away now. Can you see anything?"

George rolled down the window and peered into the night, protecting her face from the biting wind with her hand. The sleet had stopped, so visibility had improved, but the sky was black with the promise of more. She stared out across the barren fields, straining to see any sign of the train. "Listen," she whispered. "Is that the wind I'm hearing or the Midnight Flyer?" The truck's powerful engine blurred the night sounds, and George involuntarily closed her eyes, as if shutting off her sight would make her hearing more acute. "It's the horn! I'm sure! I can't see it yet, but I can hear it!"

She felt the truck lurch forward as Nancy pressed down on the gas pedal, racing against the lonely wail of the train's siren. They rode in silence, each girl intent on the job at hand.

"I can see the headlight now," George said calmly.

Nancy glanced to her right. From miles down the track, the sweeping white light of the train's headlight swung across the dark fields, disappearing into the dark sky, only to reappear on the ground seconds later. "We're close," she said. "Look! Up ahead!"

George stared down the two-lane road. A feeble red glow came from the taillights of a vehicle on the tracks, and both girls knew, even without being close enough to identify it, that the car belonged to Kamla.

"I don't see a police car," Nancy said. And then to herself, "Oh, please, Sam, have one on the way!" Her heart thudded in her chest as she fought to keep the big truck on the icy pavement. Increased speed had also increased the loss of traction. "George, time to call 911. Get us an ambulance and a squad car."

"Right!" George picked up Duke's new cellular phone from the tray and completed the call quickly. "Lucky for us he has this new toy," she said.

"There's another car up there," Nancy said, "on the other side of the tracks." She pointed at two large red taillights that shone like beacons compared to Kamla's. "A big car. Look at the exhaust. Motor's running, lights are on!"

"Shelley's goons," George muttered.

"Yes, and those sleazebags are going to take

off—once they're sure their plan is going to work."

"Their plan *isn't* going to work," George said, unfastening her seat belt. She made sure the door was unlocked and gripped the handle firmly. "I'm ready."

The train itself was visible now, still several miles down the track, but approaching relentlessly, with its circling white light casting an eerie glow on the landscape and its haunting siren piercing the frigid air.

"They're pulling away!" Nancy yelled. "They saw our lights coming at them!"

"Nan!" George's voice was a whisper, as she stared at the approaching train. "It's coming too fast! We're not going to make it."

"Yes, we are!" Nancy said grimly, glancing at the train. "Don't get out! Belt up!" Her voice dropped to a whisper. "I hope they've belted Kamla in."

George held her breath and fastened her seat belt while Nancy slowed the truck enough to maneuver it into position behind the small gray car on the tracks. The truck's reduction in speed seemed to magnify the acceleration of the train, which was bearing down on them.

"Brace yourself, George, we're going across!"

With teeth clenched in determination, and both hands tightly gripping the wheel, Nancy stepped on the gas, aiming straight for the back bumper of Kamla's car.

Chapter

Sixteen

ONLY THEIR SEAT BELTS kept Nancy and George from hitting the windshield as the truck slammed into the small car, pushing it ahead of them to safety on the other side of the tracks. The back end of the big truck shimmied with the rush of air created as the Midnight Flyer roared through.

Nancy laid her head down on the wheel. "Made it," she whispered. "Are you okay?"

"I'm okay. My nerves will never be the same, but I'm okay." With a trembling hand, George reached for the door handle. "Let's get Kamla."

Kamla's car had veered off to the right on impact and was perched on the edge of a drainage ditch, its damaged rear end badly crumpled.

Nancy ran to the driver's side door and

wrenched it open. Kamla was propped up behind the steering wheel and had been belted in. Her face was drained of color, and a bump was forming on her forehead where, Nancy assumed, her head had flopped forward and hit the wheel. She was very still.

"Is she—" George couldn't bring herself even to ask the question.

Nancy felt for a pulse. It was there, weak but steady. "She's alive," she said, nodding.

"I'll get a blanket," George said, running back to the truck.

Nancy took Kamla's small icy hand between both of hers, rubbing it to give warmth. Then she unfastened the seat belt and lifted Kamla so that George could wrap a blanket around her. Together, they carried Kamla to the warmth of the truck and laid her out on the seat and waited for the ambulance to arrive.

"I'll get her purse and personal stuff out of the car," Nancy said. "The police will have it towed as evidence. The truck has only a little dent."

Leaving George with Kamla, Nancy walked the short distance to the car. The overhead light wasn't working, so she slid in under the steering wheel and felt around on the passenger side for a handbag. Kamla's large tapestry bag was on the floor, and Nancy grasped the bone handles and pulled it up to the seat. That was when she heard it.

A cough. A short muted raspy cough. Just one. Almost like someone clearing his throat. The sound was coming from the backseat.

Nancy leapt out of the car and pushed the release on the seat, tilting it forward. And then she stood, staring down at the small, crumpled figure on the floor. Tears spilled down her cheeks as she turned back to the truck.

"I need another blanket!" she yelled to George. "Jeremy's in the car! Hurry!"

In moments George was at the car. She and Nancy debated lifting Jeremy from the floor to the backseat but decided to tuck a blanket around him and leave him where he was.

"He didn't have a seat belt on," George said, frowning. "If he was on the seat and thrown to the floor on impact, he may have broken bones."

Nancy nodded. "Yes, but he's alive! That's the important thing."

"I wish that ambulance would come," George said. "I'm going back to Kamla."

"I'll stay here," Nancy said, nodding.

Jeremy coughed again, and Nancy reached in and took his hand.

"Jeremy," she said, "it's Nancy Drew, and we have an ambulance on the way. Can you hear me?"

Jeremy stirred slightly, and his eyes fluttered open. "What's the password?" he mumbled.

"You *can* hear me!" Nancy said. "Oh, Jeremy! We'll have you out of here soon, I promise."

As she spoke, the wail of a distant siren sounded, and far down the road, Nancy could see the flashing lights of the approaching emergency vehicles. "They're coming. Are you okay?"

"My arm hurts," Jeremy said, "but I'm okay. I'm glad you're here, Nancy."

"Me, too," Nancy said, patting his head.

It didn't take long for the paramedics to load Kamla and Jeremy for the trip to the hospital. After giving their report to the officers who arrived at the same time, George and Nancy got into the truck and drove back to town.

"Do you mind if I go by the police station?" Nancy asked. "I want to give Sam an update."

"Only if they have a cafeteria," George said.

"That's right! I guess we didn't eat," Nancy replied. "Well, they do have one. And it's probably the only one in town open at this hour."

It was after two in the morning when Nancy steered into the station parking lot, but it could have been noon. All three floors of the building were lit up, and she had to wait for a car to leave before she could park. They asked for Sam at the desk, and the duty officer checked his log.

"He's down in the cafeteria," he said.

"Let's find him," George said, clutching her stomach and heading for the stairwell. "I don't think I can hold on much longer."

Grinning at George's theatrics, Nancy followed.

Sam was at a table with John Spanos when they

143

came in and, with a surprised glance, he motioned them over. Dark circles from lack of sleep ringed his eyes, and his mouth was taut. As Nancy reached the table, he managed a weak smile, but she could tell it had been a rough night for him. "Sam," she said, "Jeremy's safe! And so is Kamla!"

Sam got up so fast his chair fell over.

"They've been taken to the hospital," Nancy continued. "Jeremy was in Kamla's car. The paramedics say they'll be okay."

Sam stared at her as if she was speaking Greek, and then grabbed her around the waist and swung her around in a circle. "Hallelujah!" he yelled, beaming at George and the other officer.

Breathless, but still grinning, Sam planted a big kiss square on Nancy's lips, plopped her down in a chair, and pulled out a chair for George.

"If I sit down," George said, smiling at Sam, "I'll be too weak to get up. I'm heading that way first." She pointed to the cafeteria along the wall. "Can I bring anybody anything?"

Sam shook his head. "Got mine," he said, indicating his tray.

"I'm on my way back upstairs," Spanos said, getting up. "But thanks. Sure is nice to get some good news around here once in a while."

"A big bowl of soup and a roll, please," Nancy said. As George headed for the line, Nancy grinned at Sam. "Who goes first?" she asked.

"You can," he said, squeezing her hand.

He listened intently as she related the events of the evening.

"We were pretty sure they were going to kill Kamla at Brady Crossing, but we had no idea when we headed out there that Jeremy would be in the car, too," Nancy concluded, shaking her head at the memory of the close call. "Now it's your turn," she said to him. "Tell me what happened at the drop site."

"I really thought we'd blown it," he said, shaking his head. "Nan, you can't believe how I felt when we didn't get Jeremy."

She squeezed his hand reassuringly. "But you did get Shelley Lawson?" she asked.

"Oh, yes. We picked up Shelley Lawson and Frank Devine, but they didn't have the boy, and we couldn't get anything out of them. They just weren't talking. I don't know how she thought her scheme would work if she didn't have Jeremy to exchange for the money. But she didn't want Jeremy around to spill the beans about her, and I guess she thought we'd surrender the money anyway out of fear for his safety."

Nancy nodded, knowing how distressed Sam must have been.

"That is one professional outfit that woman runs," Sam went on. "Would you believe she was in a floatplane waiting upriver. Best as we can figure, they were going to take the small plane to

Montreal and then get on a commercial flight. We found tickets in her purse for a flight from Montreal to an island in the Caribbean."

George arrived with their food and sat down to listen.

"Nan, I apologize," Sam continued. "If I'd had a car easily available I would have sent it out there, but there were so many emergencies tonight, we didn't have enough people to cover them all. And the train dispatcher said the storm was interfering with their radios. He also said it would be a big deal to stop a freight train going at that speed, and so he wanted us to be certain . . ." Sam's voice trailed off as he spoke of the harrowing night.

"It's not your fault," Nancy reassured him. "We were running out of time. I knew we had to get to that crossing before the train. It turned out okay. We called 911, and a squad car came with the ambulance." She paused. "One other thing. Shelley's men were at the crossing when we approached. Maybe the man named Bert or Ken, or both. I don't know the make of car they had."

"We'll track it," Sam said. "We have two eyewitnesses now in Kamla and Jeremy. That will help. They should be able to clear up some of our questions." He pushed his chair back. "I have to get back upstairs," he said. "Did someone call Edwin Wright about Jeremy?"

George nodded. "The officers at the scene said they would. What will happen to Wright?"

"That's up to the district attorney."

"Oh, Sam, one other thing. Have somebody search the Olympia office building for a janitor who may be locked in a closet or something."

The next morning, Nancy followed George, who was driving the truck over to Duke's place.

"Whoa!" he said when he came out and saw the bumper. "You ladies are into a streak of bad luck, what with a stolen battery and now this. 'Course with that weather last night, I can understand you slidin' into something. But that sure looks like a pretty hard slide."

George bit back a grin.

"Got yourself a new battery, I see," Duke said to Nancy, nodding toward the Mustang. "Hope this one sticks around awhile."

"Me, too," Nancy said. "Thanks again for the loan of your truck last night. It was literally a lifesaver. And I'm sorry for the bumper damage, but my insurance will cover it."

"Accidents will happen," Duke said.

"The most deliberate accident I've ever seen," George said to Nancy as she slipped into the passenger seat of the Mustang. "But worth it. Where now? The hospital?"

When they arrived at Kamla's room in River Heights General, it looked as though a party was in full swing. Baskets of cut flowers and a huge balloon bouquet decorated the room, and excited chatter drifted out to the hall. Jodi Fontaine was sitting by Kamla's bed, and Jeremy, with his arm in a cast supported by a bright red sling, was sitting cross-legged on the bed. Sam was standing off to one side, holding a clipboard.

"Nancy! George! Come in," Kamla said when she saw them in the doorway. She introduced Jodi, who hugged both of them.

"I can never thank you enough," Jodi said, barely able to keep back the tears, "for saving the two most precious people in my life. You both deserve a medal of honor."

Kamla, looking pale but happy, echoed her thanks. Jeremy merely stared at them both and said, "I knew all along that you'd find me."

"Thanks for the vote of confidence," Nancy said. "How's the arm?"

"Cool," he said, admiring his sling. "Doesn't hurt now. At least not much."

Sam grinned at Nancy and reached down for his briefcase. "Do you mind if I conduct a little business?" he asked Kamla, snapping it open. "I brought some photos for you and Jeremy to look at. This is informal. We'll have a lineup for you down at the station when you're released, but this would be helpful for me." He divided a stack of photos in two groups and handed one to Kamla and one to Jeremy. "Just take a look through these and see if anybody looks familiar. You can trade stacks when you're done."

When they were through making selections, Nancy and George were asked to go through the same procedure. All four of them picked the same photos: Shelley Lawson, the men known as Frank and Bert, the phony janitor, Ken, and Jack Farmer.

A nurse came to take Jeremy for some tests, much to his displeasure, and Nancy and George promised to visit him before they left. Before she left, the nurse shyly asked Jodi for her autograph.

"Gladly," Jodi said, beaming up at her.

"Actually, I'm glad Jeremy had something scheduled," Nancy said as they left the room. "I wanted to ask Jodi some questions." She turned to the actress. "Does he know that Farmer was murdered?"

"Yes, I told him this morning," Jodi said. "He has an appointment with the staff psychologist later today. He realizes that he was in a very serious situation, and I'll see that he has help in working through his emotions."

"That's good," said Nancy. "I was concerned about him." She turned to Kamla. "I'm feeling relieved that the two of you were together, even though it was a terrible situation."

Kamla smiled. "But we didn't know about each other," she said. "They came to my apartment and banged on the door, saying they were the police, so I let them in. Then they made me call the school and say I was sick. And then they took me to that vacant office in the Olympia Building."

George nodded. "That's where Nancy picked up your hair scarf. They took us there, too."

Kamla reached up and pushed a lock of dark hair back from her forehead. "They gave me a shot of something," she continued, "and that was the last time I was conscious. I never saw Jeremy, and I don't think he ever saw me."

Nancy sighed. "I assume they took the knife that killed Farmer from your apartment."

"Yes. Actually they made *me* take it so it would have my fingerprints on it. And they took the bracelet right off me. At the time I didn't know why, but Detective Fanelli says they left it in the motel room where Jeremy was, hoping to lead the investigation to me."

Nancy winked at Sam. "Well, you have Shelley and Frank. Two out of four's not bad."

"Four out of four before long," Sam said. "Jeremy memorized the license number of Bert's car. He's going to use it for his next password. Bert and Ken picked him up at the motel."

"One last question," Nancy said, turning to Jodi. "The message you left on Kamla's answering machine—you said something about it all falling into place so neatly and you'd be seeing Kamla soon."

Jodi nodded. "I know. It was so innocent and it sounded so incriminating. You see, Kamla and I had planned to take Jeremy and Darcy, his friend from school, to Florida on spring break.

We were going to spend a week at one of the theme parks." She looked over at Kamla. "I hope we can still do it," she said. "I have custody during holidays, and it's okay with his father."

"What's happened with Edwin Wright?" George asked. "That sleaze."

"The district attorney has filed charges," Sam replied, grinning at George. "I agree with your description. Right now he's been released on his own recognizance, and it will be up to the court to decide what happens to him. But my hope is that they'll throw the book at him. The feeling around the department is that he should be prosecuted to the full extent of the law." He put the photos back into the briefcase and snapped it shut. "Well, time to get back to the office."

"We have to go, too," Nancy said.

Jodi put up her hand. "Wait a minute," she said. "Before you go, I want to invite all of you to join me for dinner tomorrow night. The hospital says Jeremy and Kamla will probably be released by then. Jeremy's going to bring Darcy, and I wondered if you"—she looked at George—"if you'd like to invite your friend with the truck. Without even being on the scene, he played a big part in this happy ending."

George smiled. "How do you feel about ten-gallon hats and cowboy boots?" she asked.

"Might just wear some myself," Jodi drawled. "We can go to the Barbecue House."

"You're on," George said.

Nancy and Sam nodded their agreement.

"Speaking of happy endings," Nancy said, as she waved good-bye to Kamla and Jodi, "this whole episode sounds like a good movie script to me!"

Nancy's next case:

Naval flight trainee Jill Parker died in a fiery crash at Florida's Davis Field, and the base commander has asked Nancy to go undercover to investigate. Officially, the incident has been listed as an accident. But off the record, the evidence points to sabotage. Nancy finds that the atmosphere is charged with danger . . . in more ways than one! One of her top suspects is fellow trainee Crash Beauford—brazen, arrogant, and devastatingly attractive. Crash has Nancy in his sights, and he rarely misses. But she's determined to keep her eye on the course. She's zeroing in on a killer, and at these speeds and at these heights, a single distraction could lead to disaster . . . in *Flying Too High,* Case #106 in The Nancy Drew Files™.